BAKER'S DOZEN

IMA COME HOME

BAKER'S DOZEN

IMA COME HOME

Created by Miriam Zakon
Written by Aidel Stein

Targum/Feldheim

First published 1993

Copyright © 1993 by Targum Press
ISBN 1-56871-009-7

Phototypeset at Targum Press

Printing plates by Frank, Jerusalem

Published by:
Targum Press Inc.
22700 W. Eleven Mile Rd.
Southfield, Mich. 48034

Distributed by:
Feldheim Publishers
200 Airport Executive Park
Spring Valley, N.Y. 10977

Distributed in Israel by:
Targum Press Ltd.
POB 43170
Jerusalem 91430

Printed in Israel

Contents

WHO'S WHO IN THE BAKER'S DOZEN

ASHER BAKER, *age 16. The eldest of the Baker clan, Ashi dorms in a nearby yeshivah — but still manages to take part in the family's adventures!*

BRACHA BAKER, *age 13. It's not easy being the oldest girl in such a large family, especially when you've got five famous sisters just two years younger than you are! But Bracha always rises to the challenge, usually with a smile. Her hobbies are reading, gardening (with her mother), and painting.*

RIVKA BAKER, *age 11. Eldest of the quintuplets, Rivka often tries to mother — and sometimes tries to boss around — her sisters. A talented guitar player with a beautiful voice.*

ZAHAVA BAKER, *age 11. With eleven brothers and sisters, Zahava still manages to get her way. A pretty girl, the kind who gets picked to play Queen Esther in Purim plays, she is usually good-natured, but sometimes high-strung. Her hobbies are drawing, fashion, and needlepoint.*

DINA BAKER, *age 11. Dini is as dependable as her sister Zahava is flighty. She hates injustice and defends the underdog in any fight. Her hobbies include reading and dancing.*

TIKVA BAKER, *age 11. Tikva is blind in one eye and has very poor eyesight in the other; still, she is fiercely independent. Though she cannot see at all in the dark, she refuses to walk with a cane. A very bright girl, she reads all her books in braille. She is shy and reserved with strangers, but at home everyone looks to her for advice and support. Tikva writes poetry in her spare time.*

YOCHEVED BAKER, *age 11. "The Baby Dynamo," as her father calls her, is the smallest of the quints, and a ball of energy and excitement. Yochie's always ready for adventure, quick to anger but quick to forgive. She loves schemes, the more outrageous the better, but rarely thinks about consequences until she's up to her neck in them. Her hobbies change with every new month.*

MOISHY BAKER, *age 9. "He's his father's genius, and my gray hairs," is the way Mrs. Baker describes her difficult prodigy. When he's in the mood, he can memorize hundreds of mishnayos; when he doesn't feel like it, he can fail every math test his teacher gives him. He collects coins and is a computer whiz.*

CHEZKY BAKER, *age 8. A jolly boy, always laughing, terrible in his studies but so good-natured about it that even his teachers have to smile. An expert softball player.*

DONNY BAKER, *age 5. A tough cookie, an independent kid who doesn't care what anyone else thinks of him.*

SARALEH BAKER, *age 3. A sweet little girl, with a dangerous tendency to wandering off.*

RACHEL AHUVA BAKER, *age 1. A fat baby, all cheeks and tummy and legs. She's usually smiling — and why not, with four fathers and seven mothers (besides Abba and Ima)?*

1
"Where's Ima?"

I think just about the last kind of club I'd want to join is a sewing club!" Yochie exclaimed as a March wind blew her through the kitchen door. She dropped her book bag on the floor and pushed her disheveled hair out of her expressive brown eyes.

"Not my kind of club either!" said Moishy from his seat at the kitchen table.

The rest of the Baker quintuplets sailed in after Yochie, talking all at once.

"Just because you don't like sewing doesn't mean it isn't worthwhile," her sister Dina said seriously as she walked through the kitchen.

"I didn't mean it that way," Yochie shouted after her.

"Yochie," said Rivka, the oldest quint, "I almost tripped over your book bag!"

"Sorry, boss!" Yochie grinned at her sister, grabbed her book bag, and dashed up the stairs.

"She always does that," said Tikva, giving her sister a knowing look through her thick glasses. "It's best to just detour around the sink."

"I guess that's a good idea," Rivka sighed. She perked up and looked at Zahava, who was standing by the door, arms crossed. "I want to know more about the Sewing Club, even if other people don't." She glared at Moishy, who was sitting quietly, enjoying the goings on.

"Me, too!" Dina added coming back into the kitchen.

"Okay, I do, too," Yochie admitted, coming in right after Dina. "Not that I want to sew," she added quickly. "I just like to know what's going on." The girls looked at Zahava expectantly.

Zahava slowly uncrossed her arms, smoothed her long brown hair, and straightened her blouse. With great dignity, she sat down at the table and cleared her throat.

"It has been decided that it would be beneficial for the Bais Yaakov of Bloomfield to have a Sewing Club. The purpose of the club would be to bring together girls who are interested in sewing in order to exchange ideas, improve skills, encourage beginners, and work on worthwhile projects," she said, counting off on her fingers.

"Laudable," commented Moishy.

"Nobody asked you!" Zahava snapped.

"Really, Moishy," added Dina. "Can't you just listen?"

"Actually, 'laudable' means praiseworthy," Tikva

said quietly. "A good thing to do."

"Oh." Zahava blushed. "Sorry."

"Double sorry," said Dina.

"No problem," said Moishy cheerfully. "Do go on."

"Anyway," Zahava continued. "Mrs. Greenstein, Elisheva's mother, who works in the fashion industry, will be our advisor, and Mrs. Pearl, the Home Ec. teacher, will help us. Fraidie Glass from the eighth grade was voted president, and guess who is the assistant head?" She took a deep breath.

"Idy Bodner?" Moishy guessed.

"Oh, Moishy!" Zahava let out all her breath at once. "Where's Ima?" she asked suddenly.

"Out somewhere," Moishy informed her. "She left a note saying that she'll be a little late." He held out a piece of paper. Rivka snatched it. All of the quints crowded around her to read the note.

Dear kids,

Welcome home! I'm sorry I'm not there. I'm at a meeting and I'll be a little late. Rachel Ahuva and Saraleh are at Great-Aunt Freida's — if I'm not back by 5:00, please pick them up. Donny is at the Erlangers — Baruch's mother will drive him home.

A casserole is in the oven. Please turn it on at 5:15. Do your usual chores, and I'll be home sooner than you know!

Love you all,
Ima

"Oh!" Zahava cried in disappointment. "And I wanted to tell her that I was chosen assistant head!"

"Oh, wow!" exclaimed Tikva. "Assistant head, mazal tov!"

"I had news to tell, too," said Moishy.

"I wonder where she is?" Tikva asked.

"Some meeting or another," sang Yochie blithely. "It says so on the note."

"She just finished illustrating that book on Sukkos," Dina said. "Maybe it's about that."

"Or a new project," put in Rivka.

"I guess so," said Tikva, but she felt vaguely uneasy. Ima had been gone quite a lot lately. It wasn't like her! Mentally shaking herself, she looked at Zahava.

"...and I'm sure we'll be able to come up with some very worthwhile projects," Zahava was saying. She eyed her sisters critically. "Just dressing this family would be a worthwhile project."

"What do you mean?" Yochie asked innocently.

"Just look at all of you. Rivka, that skirt is hopelessly out of style. Yochie's blouse is torn, and Dina is wearing the drabbest colors. And Tikki, must you always be so conservative?"

Moishy snorted.

"And you," Zahava turned on him. "Those pants must have belonged to Ashi!" she said, referring to their oldest brother. Ashi, seven years older than Moishy, was away in yeshiva.

"And if they did?" Moishy asked defensively.

Zahava crossed her arms and sniffed. Just then Bracha, the oldest Baker girl, walked in. Zahava turned on her.

"And you could really do something else with your hair." She pointed to her sister's head.

"What?" Bracha was bewildered. "I've just been out in the wind."

"Never mind, Bracha," said Dina. "Zahava is just up on her podium again."

"I guess this has to do with the Sewing Club," said Bracha. "Fraidie told me all about it on the way home. She's really glad to have you as her assistant. Congratulations!"

"Thank you." Zahava looked pleased. "It's good that at least one Baker has some fashion sense."

"Now, look here..." Rivka began.

"I think we'd better start getting dinner ready," Tikva interrupted.

"Where's Ima?" Bracha asked.

"She's out." Moishy handed her the note. The rest of the family went soberly about their business.

Zahava went to make the salad. As she cleaned the lettuce, she thought about how pretty the green leaves were. But you'd have to be a redhead to get away with wearing this color, she decided.

Zahava was lost in thought. I guess I shouldn't have shouted at Bracha that way just when she walked into the house, she chided herself. Zahava didn't always get along with her older sister but she loved and respected her. She wished she could be as good a student. She saw how hard it must be to be the oldest sister with the quints always in the spotlight. Bracha really could stand on her own as a special person. She's smart, funny, and really responsible. Zahava wrinkled her nose. I wish she'd do something different with her hair, though.

Rivka walked by Zahava without a word. Maybe I shouldn't have spoken that way to her either, Zahava admitted to herself. Because she's the oldest quint, she thinks she's in charge. She is a good leader. But why does she have to be so bossy? And I'll get rid of that awful skirt she's wearing, if I have to burn it...*bli neder*.

"Do you need help with that salad?"

Zahava jumped. "Tikva!" she exclaimed. "I didn't hear you coming!"

"Just call me pussyfoot," Tikva grinned at her. "Do you need help?"

"No thanks."

"Good," said Tikva. "Yochie and I are going to get the little girls."

"See ya'."

Zahava took some tomatoes out of the vegetable bin in the refrigerator and began to wash them. Tikki is so wonderful, she thought. Legally blind and she never complains. I don't think I could do it. And good old Yochie. She can be a real nutcase, but she's so caring underneath.

Moishy came into the kitchen for the silverware.

That Moishy, Zahava thought. The Mad Genius!

How was I supposed to know what "laudable" means?

"Why are you staring at me?" Moishy asked her. "Should I go up and change my pants?"

"Oh, Moishy!" On impulse she asked him, "What was your news for Ima?"

Moishy's expression visibly brightened. "There's going to be a Science Fair in school," he said. "I'm going to enter. I have a great idea for some software, a terrific game that's good for learning, too. The idea is..." They both turned suddenly at a noise coming from the kitchen window.

"Chezky!" they shouted. Leave it to athletic Chezky to climb up to the kitchen window.

Eight-year-old Chezky waved at them and disappeared. He reappeared at the kitchen door and banged into the house, the wind slamming the door behind him. His *kippah* was hanging precariously on the side of his soft brown hair, and there was a smudge on his nose from the window. His cheeks were red from the blustery weather. "Where's Ima?" he asked.

"The big question," Moishy quipped.

"She's late," Zahava informed him.

"Oh." Chezky looked disappointed. "Well, I guess she'll be back soon."

"Laudable optimism," Moishy nodded sagely.

"Yep," Chezky agreed and went to the refrigerator for an apple.

"You know what that means?" Zahava demanded. While Chezky was one of the most cheerful kids around, and really fun to be with, he was certainly not the smartest.

Chezky said a *berachah* and took a bite of his apple. "Look," he said. "Moishy's not going to say anything lousy about me out of the blue, so why shouldn't I agree?" He started out of the kitchen. At the door he turned. "Besides," he said, "Moishy told me what it meant on the way home!" He winked at her and slipped out.

Tikva and Yochie returned with Saraleh and Rachel Ahuva on their backs.

"Why are you carrying them?" Zahava asked.

"We forgot the stroller and didn't want to go back for it," Yochie admitted. "So when we started to carry the baby, Saraleh wanted a ride, too!" Rachel Ahuva opened her big, round eyes wide and laughed.

"We flew in the wind!" Saraleh bounced on her sister's back in three-year-old fashion, gold curls bobbing.

"Whoa!" shouted Yochie and gently let her little sister down. "Still no Ima?" she asked.

"Still no Ima," Zahava replied.

Five-year-old Donny arrived soon afterward, but still no Ima. The children did their homework and played in a subdued manner.

Right on time, Mr. Baker came in the door, but still no Ima.

"Abba, what is taking Ima so long?" Bracha asked as she took her father's raincoat.

"Yeah," Donny demanded, clenching his small fists. "If she doesn't hurry, she'll miss dinner."

Mr. Baker laughed his deep laugh, his smile peeking out of his thick beard, his round cheeks making large cherries under his twinkling eyes. "It looks like she will miss dinner," he said, taking his small son's hand and leading him toward the dining room. "She told me that we should start without her. Is dinner ready?"

Yochie popped up next to them. "Yes-it-is-but-where-is-Ima?" she said quickly.

"Yes, where is she?" clamored several other children.

"I'm not quite sure," Mr. Baker teased. "Maybe she went to see a man about a horse?"

"Abba!" the children groaned.

"Let's wash and sit down. The mystery lady will probably show up by then." He went into the kitchen to wash up.

"What lady?" asked Saraleh.

"He meant Ima," Donny informed her.

"Ima's a lady?" Saraleh asked.

After the family was seated and the food served, the children tried again to get their father to tell them what Ima was doing. Mr. Baker remained mysteriously uninformative.

"You'll find out soon enough," he said. He then turned to Moishy and firmly changed the subject. "What's new with you?"

"There's going to be a Science Fair in school," Moishy informed him.

Mr. Baker's eyes lit up. Although he worked as a

t attorney, in his spare time he was an inventor.

"Have you cooked something up?" he asked.

"I have a great idea, a computer game — fun and educational. I have most of the programming worked out, and Ashi is going to help me with the rest. I already asked him. The other kids are going to do the usual stuff, you know, volcanos and ringing bells. I'm pretty sure I can win first prize..."

"Don't count your chickens," Yochie intoned.

"Oh, come on, Yochie," said Moishy. "How could an old volcano win over some really good software?"

"You're not the only raving genius around!" she returned.

"Yochie!" her father warned.

"It's just his snobby attitude..." but Yochie stopped talking under her father's steady gaze.

"It sounds very interesting, Moishy. We all wish you the best of luck," said Mr. Baker.

Just then, Ima walked in.

"Ima!" the children cried.

"Where were you?"

"Oh, Ima, wait until I tell you about the Sewing Club!"

"What took you so long?"

"I have this great idea for the Science Fair..."

"Why are you so late?"

"What is going on? Abba won't tell us anything!"

Mr. Baker stood up. "Quiet!" he said. "Let your mother wash up and sit down. Give her a moment to breathe!"

"Oh, sorry, Ima!"

"Here's your chair, Ima!"

"Can I get you a drink, Ima?"

"You must be starving," said Bracha, heaping a plate high with food.

"Shh!" said Donny out loud to no one in particular.

Mrs. Baker sat down in her chair and proudly surveyed her lively brood. They might be a double handful and then some, but they gave her plenty of *nachas*. They watched her as she ate, holding back their curiosity.

After a few minutes, she turned to Mr. Baker and asked him if he would like to tell the news.

"It's your news, you tell it," he waved at her grandly.

"Well," she began, looking over a sea of eager faces. "Everyone here knows that I work as a free-lance illustrator. That means I don't work for anyone in particular, but I take jobs as they come. Sometimes I have work and sometimes I don't. Normally this doesn't matter since, *baruch Hashem*, we've always had plenty. However, if you all remember, there was a nasty tornado not so long ago..."

"How could we forget?" interrupted Yochie. The other children voiced their agreement until their father shushed them.

"Anyway," Mrs. Baker continued, "this caused some structural damage to the house, in case no one noticed." The children laughed. "Therefore, we needed to come up with a little more money. As I was hunting around for jobs, I called up an old friend of mine from

Baltimore, Nava Schwartz. I've done some work for her before. She started a small publishing house called Sefer Press."

"Saraleh has a book from Sefer Press!" Dina exclaimed.

"The one Ima did," Rivka informed them.

"That's right," Mrs. Baker agreed. "So let me tell you how surprised I was to find out that she was moving to Bloomfield, in fact, that she is already here! The company is expanding, and her husband is opening an outlet, a bookstore, right here in Bloomfield."

"Does she have a job for you, Ima?" Bracha asked.

"She has a job for me all right, and not a free-lance job either, but a position in the company as director of the art department!" Mrs. Baker smiled and looked around at her family expectantly. There was a stunned silence.

Zahava was the first to speak. "Oh, Ima, that's great! What a chance to use all of your talents! Wow!"

"Yeah, really," said Bracha, with a hint of hesitation.

"What will your hours be?" Moishy asked suspiciously.

"Hours, shmours!" Zahava said to him. "What a great opportunity!"

"I'll be in charge of the entire art department. I'll practically be my own boss. I'll be in charge of layout, cover design, hiring artists..."

"What will your hours be?" Moishy asked again.

"Who will take care of us?" asked Donny.

Donny's worried face brought Mrs. Baker back down to earth. "Don't worry *zeeskeit*, I'm not going away, I'm just going to work."

"We'll be redoing the chore list so that everyone can pitch in and help," said Mr. Baker.

"Even Abba," Mrs. Baker said.

"Even Abba, wow!" Chezky exclaimed.

"Hush, Chezky," Dina shushed him.

"It will mean a little more work for all of us, but we can't let this opportunity slide by. I know that the Baker family will rally around and pitch in." Mr. Baker smiled at them encouragingly.

"What will your hours be?" Moishy asked again.

Mrs. Baker sighed. "We figure that the beginning will be the hardest. After the first three months, when there is an established infrastructure, I'll be able to cut my hours drastically."

Undeterred, Moishy asked, "And until then?"

"I'll be working more or less full-time."

"Oh."

"Now aren't we proud of Ima? Not everyone could land this job!" said Mr. Baker.

The children voiced their enthusiasm and bombarded their mother with questions. Still, beneath the excitement they were uneasy. Ima at work? Extra helping out? It didn't take much to see that things were going to be very different around the Baker house soon. And they didn't know if they liked that at all.

2
Life without Mother

P sst! Psst! Zahava, wake up!"

"Hmm?" Zahava turned over from her stomach to her back and put her arm over her eyes.

"Zahava, wake up, now!"

Zahava slowly opened her eyes and tried to focus on the face hovering over her. It was Bracha. "What time is it?" she asked sleepily.

"It's 6:30," Bracha answered. "Now wake up!"

"Are you out of your mind? I never get out of bed until seven o'clock." Zahava turned back over onto her stomach and put her head under her pillow.

Bracha pulled up the corner of the pillow and whispered fiercely into her sister's ear. "Don't you remember? Today is Ima's first day of work, and it's our turn to get up early and help. Are you awake now?"

"Aaaeeeow...yes," Zahava yawned.

"So get dressed and come and help me." Bracha went quickly out of the room.

Zahava looked over at the clock on the desk. "Six thirty-two — I don't believe it. What normal person would get up at this hour?" She gathered her clothing and tiptoed out of the room.

After dressing, Zahava looked into the mirror to do her hair. There, she thought. With a little effort you can look nice even in a school uniform. She leaned toward the mirror to have a closer look. The blue lines under my eyes match my skirt, she thought grimly. Oh, no! I brought the wrong hair ribbon! I must have picked out the wrong color in the dark! There is no way that I am wearing this ribbon with these clothes! She turned and stalked out of the bathroom.

"Zahava, there you are!" Mrs. Baker rushed down the hall with Rachel Ahuva in her arms. "Here, hold the baby. I would have given her to your father but he went to an earlier minyan so he could be back to help. I have to finish getting dressed, and then I have to finish the sandwiches!" Mrs. Baker thrust the baby into Zahava's arms and dashed away.

"Ima, just let me change my..." Zahava began. "Now what will I do?" she asked her tiny sister.

Rachel Ahuva, unused to the early hour and wanting her mother, began to cry. Zahava frantically tried to hush her.

Moishy poked his head out of his room. "Do you know what time it is?" he demanded.

"Six thirty-seven," Zahava quipped and fled downstairs.

In the kitchen, she found Bracha setting the table for breakfast. Zahava looked at her in disbelief. "Frosted Flakes? Fruit Loops? That's Donny and Saraleh food. We only have that stuff in an emergency!"

"I guess this is an emergency," said Bracha. "Ima doesn't have time to make anything else, and I certainly don't. Do you?"

"No!" said Zahava quickly. She put the baby in her high chair and poured a small bowl of cereal and milk for her. The baby kept on howling.

"I hope she doesn't do this all morning at Great-Aunt Freida's!"

"Me, too." Bracha finished setting out the breakfast things. Mrs. Baker burst into the kitchen.

"Oh, Bracha, good, you finished. Zahava, what are you letting Rachel Ahuva do?" Mrs. Baker pointed to the baby, who, in her anger, slammed her hand into her cereal. The bowl flipped over and dumped on her lap. She screamed even louder. "Now she's a mess! And I have to get her to Aunt Freida's by 7:30!"

Zahava didn't know what to say. It never really made a difference how the baby ate as long as she ate something. It hadn't occurred to Zahava to try and keep the baby clean.

Mrs. Baker took the baby out of her high chair and held her at arm's length. "Here, you'll have to change her," she said, handing her to Zahava. She brushed at her sleeves. "I hope I didn't get any cereal on me."

Zahava and Bracha exchanged a look. Rachel Ahuva still screamed.

"Oh, poor baby!" Mrs. Baker cried. "Change her quickly, Zahava, so I can cuddle her before I go." She turned to Bracha. "Come, let's make the sandwiches. No, you make the sandwiches and I'll put together the casserole for supper."

Zahava held Rachel Ahuva close as she went up the stairs. The baby put her head on her sister's shoulder and sniffed. As she reached the top of the stairs, she heard the various alarm clocks of the Baker family begin to ring.

"IIIIIIIma!" Chezky hollered. "I can't find my socks!"

"IIIIIIIma, I need you to sign something!" Yochie put her head out of her bedroom. "Where's Ima?" she asked.

"Making supper," said Zahava.

"Ugh!" Yochie exclaimed. "At seven o'clock in the morning?"

Zahava went into the small girls' room to change the baby. There she found Saraleh playing with her dolls.

"Why aren't you getting dressed?" she asked her.

"I can't," Saraleh replied calmly.

"Why not?"

"I need help," said Saraleh as she put a dress on one of her dolls. Zahava took out a new outfit for the baby and began to change her.

"You seem to be doing fine with that doll," she

mentioned to Saraleh.

"Dolls are easier than me," Saraleh replied.

"Who's supposed to be helping you this morning?"

"Ima." Saraleh put another doll into a coat and shoes.

"No," Zahava corrected her. "Ima's going to work. Who's supposed to be helping you?"

"Don't know."

Zahava finished dressing the baby, stuffed the dirty clothes into the hamper, and turned to Saraleh again.

"Why don't you at least take off your pajamas or something?"

"I can't." Saraleh took the dress off of the first doll and put on a different one. Zahava sighed and left the room.

On her way down the hall she remembered the hair ribbon. Still lugging Rachel Ahuva, she went back down the hall. The bedroom that she shared with her sisters was full of the usual early morning activity.

"I had to practically stuff the pen into Ima's hand to get her to sign this note," Yochie was saying.

"She must be very busy," said Tikva thoughtfully.

"I guess so..." Yochie spun around to Zahava. "Hi, early bird, catch any worms?"

"Oh yuck, Yochie!" Zahava went over to her dresser and opened the drawer with one hand. She took out another hair ribbon while trying to keep Rachel Ahuva's pudgy fingers out of her possessions.

"Zahava, look at you!" Rivka pointed to her blouse. "You can't go to school like that!"

Zahava looked. Smeared down her front and one shoulder was cold cereal and milk. "Oh no!" she wailed. "Oh, I don't believe it! I have to change!" Zahava put the baby down on the rug and ran to her closet. "What am I going to wear!" she wailed.

Moishy burst into the room. "Ima says that you have to help me find my socks!"

"Who?" Dina asked him.

"Zahava."

Zahava whirled around. "What? Are you out of your mind? Go and find your own socks." She turned back to her closet.

"It's your turn this morning and you have to help me!"

Zahava glared at her younger brother, then stalked out of the room and charged down the hall and into the laundry. There, in the "to be folded" basket, were a mountain of socks. She remembered her mother starting to sort them last night and then being called to the phone. Rummaging through the pile, throwing socks right and left, she finally found a pair for Moishy. She stomped down the hall, threw open the door of his room, tossed the socks inside, and slammed the door shut. Then, once again, she charged back to her room and continued to sort through her wardrobe for something to wear.

"Zahava, where is the baby?" Mrs. Baker called from downstairs. Zahava looked at Rachel Ahuva, who had finally stopped crying and was playing happily on the rug.

"Here!" she called back. She held up two blouses.

"Bring her downstairs right now, please!"

Zahava's hands tightened convulsively on the blouses. With great effort she dropped them, picked up the baby, and ran down the stairs. Her mother was in the kitchen, by the sink. Her father was on his hands and knees wiping up the spilt cereal.

"Abba, what are you doing down there?" Zahava asked.

"Trying to be useful," Mr. Baker grunted.

"There you are!" said Mrs. Baker. She wiped her hands and held them out for the baby. "Just help me with the portacrib; Rachel Ahuva will use it at Aunt Freida's for her nap."

"Ima, isn't there someone else to do it?" Zahava looked around her desperately. "I have to change my clothing. I can't..."

"Zahava," her mother said impatiently, "there isn't time."

Zahava swallowed hard, picked up the crib, and followed her mother out to the car. She thought she would explode as her mother strapped the baby into the car seat, put the baby bag into the car next to her, and finally put the portacrib in the back. "Bye, Ima!" Zahava dashed towards the house.

"Aren't you going to wish me luck?" Mrs. Baker asked.

"Good luck, Ima!"

"Hey, Ima's going!" Donny shouted from the house. Half-a-dozen Bakers poured out of the back door. Tikva and Dina leaned out of upstairs windows and waved enthusiastically.

"Good-bye, Ima, good-bye!"

"Good luck, Ima!"

"It should be *behatzlachah!*"

"Where's your father?" She scanned the sea of faces.

"Here, dear!" Mr. Baker hopped down the back steps.

"Listen, Ephraim, don't forget the shopping; the list is on the bulletin board. Add a couple of jars of gefilte fish, a package of crackers, extra apple juice, and some tissues to the list. Don't forget to call Great-Aunt Freida to ask if there's anything that she needs, and if you pick up the baby today don't leave the bottles there. Chezky has some sort of practice; arrange for him to get home. And don't wash the colors on hot!"

"Right!" said a bewildered Mr. Baker.

Mrs. Baker gave a few of the closest children hugs. "Good-bye *kinderlach*, I'll see you tonight! Dina, stop that, you'll fall out, *chas veshalom*. Donny, your sweater is backwards! Moishy, put on your shoes! Zahava, what is all over your shirt?"

Zahava looked down at her shirt and back at her mother again. I can't believe this is happening, she thought.

"Bye-bye, Ima," Saraleh poked her head out from

between her brothers and sisters.

"Saraleh, you're still in your pajamas!" Mrs. Baker started towards her. Bracha scooped up her sister. "Run, Ima, you'll be late! I'll take care of her!"

"Thanks, Bracha." Mrs. Baker gave a last wave and started up the car. The children jumped up and down and waved as she pulled out of the driveway and drove down the street.

"I feel like crying," said Rivka.

"Yikes!" Moishy exclaimed. "We have to go in ten minutes!" Everyone ran back into the house. Bracha dashed upstairs with Saraleh and threw her into her clothes. Chezky helped Donny turn his sweater around and choked down breakfast. Moishy ran to get his shoes. Zahava ran upstairs to change. Mr. Baker ran in circles.

When Zahava got downstairs, her brothers had already left and her sisters were waiting for her impatiently.

"I don't know why we waited..." Yochie began.

"We're going to be late!" Dina exclaimed.

Zahava turned to get her lunch bag. To her horror, the counter was empty. "Where is my lunch? Didn't anyone make me lunch?"

Bracha clapped her hand to her head. "Oh, Zahava, I'm so sorry," she said. "I was in the middle of making the lunches when Ima left, and then I had to go and dress Saraleh. I must have made one too few!"

"Now what?" Zahava cried.

"We're going to be late!" Rivka wailed.

"Don't panic," shouted Yochie. She ran to the refrigerator and grabbed a container of cottage cheese. Then she took two pieces of bread from the bread box, a banana from the bowl on the counter, and a box of juice, and stuffed them all into a paper bag. "Instant lunch!" she declared, handing the bag to Zahava with a flourish.

"Yeah, Yochie!" Tikva cried.

"Thank you, Yochie," sniffed Zahava gratefully. "Now let's get out of here!" She ran out the door followed by her sisters, who dragged a bewildered Saraleh behind them. Yochie poked her head back in the door and yelled, "Bye, Abba!"

"Good-bye!" yelled Mr. Baker from the laundry room.

After practically throwing Saraleh into her nursery school, the girls arrived at their classroom just as the bell was ringing.

After her awful morning, Zahava looked forward to getting home and relaxing after school. As the girls walked into the empty kitchen, Yochie stopped short. "Look at the kitchen table," she said.

"What's wrong with it?" Tikva asked.

"It's empty," Yochie answered.

"So?"

"It's usually full."

"The sink is full," said Dina, wrinkling her nose at the breakfast dishes.

Tikva sighed. "We'll just have to be big girls and

get out our own snack," she said. "You don't have to be so dramatic, Yochie. We haven't exactly been abandoned."

Yochie looked at her with big, forlorn eyes.

"Well, we haven't. It's pretty spoiled, really, to have a snack laid out for us every day."

"I think it's normal," Yochie sniffed. She walked into the pantry. A second later, she walked out again, a box of cookies in her hand. "Cookies and milk, anyone?"

After their snack, Zahava went to her room to plan out her first sewing project for the club.

If anyone would ask my opinion, she thought, I think we should design a new uniform. Take the colors, for instance....

"Zahava!" Bracha stood at the door of the room, impatiently tapping one foot. She was holding Saraleh in one hand and a sheet of music in the other.

"What's up?" Zahava asked.

"Aren't you supposed to be watching Saraleh?" Bracha demanded. "I found her in the kitchen eating the rest of the cookies."

Zahava stood up and put both hands on her hips. "Why do I have to watch her? Aren't we both on duty today?"

"Zahava," said Bracha patiently. "We agreed that you would watch Saraleh and I would take charge of dinner."

Zahava's hands dropped. "I'm sorry, I forgot." She held out her arms. "Come, Saraleh." Saraleh skipped to her, and Bracha left the room.

"Can I use your markers?" Saraleh asked.

Zahava, who had gone back to her planning, looked up and said, "No."

"Can I wear your Shabbos shoes?"

"No."

"Can I jump on the beds?"

"No! Just play something and leave me alone."

Saraleh gave a little sigh and sat down in a corner. She looked around the room, saw all of the things she couldn't do, and sighed again. Curling up, she tried to make herself into a ball. She tucked her arms behind her folded knees and bent her head over. Peering through her ankles, she noticed a piece of fuzz on the carpet. She pulled at it. It was attached to the carpet, so she pulled harder. It came away with a small piece of the carpet. The hole it left was full of fuzz, too, so she pulled at that fuzz. When she pulled away that fuzz, there was more fuzz behind it.

"Saraleh, what are you doing!" Zahava was standing over her with a shocked look on her face. Saraleh looked at the hole in the carpet and couldn't explain.

"Come," Zahava said, holding out her hand. "We'd better go to your room." Zahava pulled her sister to her feet, rubbed her foot over the hole until it was filled with more or less the original piece of fuzz, and led her out of the room.

When they got to the little girls' room, Saraleh made straight for her dolls. She took two of them and a pile of clothes and brought them to Zahava. "Dress them," she said.

"But I saw you dress these dolls this morning!" Zahava protested.

"Dress them. Please," Saraleh replied implacably.

Zahava looked at the doll clothes in her hand. There wasn't even anything here that matched. This was going to be one long afternoon.

When she finally escaped, she found her sisters running around preparing the salad and setting the table fore dinner.

"Well, here's the lady of leisure," said Yochie as she dashed past.

"That's what you think," Zahava groaned. "What's for dinner?"

"Casserole," said Bracha as she closed the oven. "It's almost ready. Ima should be home soon."

"Goody!" said Zahava.

"Double goody!" added Dina.

"Triple goody!" agreed Rivka.

"I hope so," said Tikva.

"What do you mean 'I hope so,' " Bracha asked her.

"Well, she'll probably be very tired..."

"Here's Ima! Here's Ima!" shouted Donny. He and Chezky were dragging Mrs. Baker through the door, followed by Mr. Baker carrying the baby.

"Ima! Ima!"

"Did you have a good day? Was it fun?"

"Zahava fixed the carpet," Saraleh announced.

"What?" asked Mrs. Baker.

"Never mind," said Zahava quickly. "You must be

starving. Let's sit down to dinner and you can tell us all about it."

The Bakers sat down, and as they ate Mrs. Baker described her office, the current projects, the artist she'd interviewed, and just how much work there was.

"I'm utterly exhausted," she said as she leaned back in her chair and closed her eyes.

"Ima, I've started my project for the Science Fair," Moishy spoke up.

"Mmmmmmmmmm," said Mrs. Baker, without opening her eyes.

"I've got to come up with a sewing idea for the club," said Zahava. "I wouldn't mind redesigning the school uniform but..."

"Mmmmmmmmmm," said Mrs. Baker.

"What's wrong with the uniform?" Dina asked.

Zahava rolled her eyes. "First of all, the colors are awful. Don't you think so, Ima?"

"Mmmmmmmmmm."

"Ima, are you awake?" Rivka asked.

"I think maybe Ima should go to bed," said Mr. Baker. Just then, the telephone rang. Moishy jumped up and got it.

"It's for you, Ima. It's your boss."

Mrs. Baker jumped up. "It must be important." She went to the kitchen telephone and began to talk animatedly. The children exchanged glances while Mr. Baker smiled indulgently.

The days that followed were more or less the same.

The mornings were a mad rush, as the children riffled through the piled-up laundry for their clothes and struggled to cope with extra chores. They sighed over memories of carrot sticks and homemade strudel as they munched their boxed cookies. Whoever watched Saraleh felt the afternoon was a loss, which often caused arguments over exactly whose turn it was to babysit. And dinner was casserole, casserole, casserole.

Mr. Baker tried to help, but somehow the phone kept ringing for him at the worst times. One night, Donny and Saraleh went to bed an hour late because Abba was on the telephone. Another day, the laundry wasn't done because Mr. Baker had a series of emergency meetings.

One afternoon, several days after Mrs. Baker started her new job, Zahava was working in the kitchen on a project for the Sewing Club. The club members bought wire frames and were making frilly light shades. On the wide kitchen table, Zahava laid out her brightly colored fabric. She had gone through the scrap bag until she found just the right colors to match her mother's home studio.

When this is finished and hung up, she said to herself, it will brighten up the whole room. It's so nice to work in a pretty room.

Zahava sighed. Not that there's been anyone working in that room lately.... She looked up and looked around the kitchen. This house is so empty without Ima here all day. I never realized how much she filled it up. Zahava thought of the dark studio, and of all of Ima's beautiful art supplies sitting in their boxes and jars, unused and forlorn.

Oh well. Zahava looked down again at her work. "There! Now all I need is some thread and I can start sewing." Zahava went into her mother's studio where the sewing supplies were kept. She rummaged through the thread box for some time before she realized that she wasn't finding what she was looking for. Oh no! she panicked. There's no red thread! What will I do?

She went back into the kitchen and looked down at her project. If Ima were here she'd know what to do, she thought. She probably put the red thread somewhere else, or she knows who has it. Then she had an inspiration. "I know!" she clapped her hands. "I'll call her!"

Zahava jumped across the kitchen to the telephone. Next to the telephone, all of the important telephone numbers were posted. Right at the bottom of the list was Ima's work number. Without hesitation, Zahava dialed and waited.

"Hello, Sefer Press," someone answered. "May I help you?"

"I'd like to speak to Mrs. Baker, please," Zahava said politely.

"Shoshana, it's for you!" the voice called her mother. Zahava felt one small butterfly in her stomach.

"Hello?" said her mother's voice.

"Hello, Ima? It's Zahava."

"Hello Zahava! Is everything okay?" Mrs. Baker

sounded worried.

"Everything's fine," Zahava reassured her. "Was that the secretary?"

"Yes," Mrs. Baker replied. "So why are you calling?"

"Ima, I'm calling because I couldn't find any red thread."

"Zahava, I don't think that qualifies as a good reason to call me at work..."

"Ima," Zahava interrupted. "I have to get this project finished soon! And there is no other color that matches!"

Mrs. Baker sighed. "Run to Mrs. Bekerman. She sews all of the time. Borrow the thread from her, and tell her I'll get it back to her as soon as I can."

"Thank you, Ima, I love you!"

"Love you too, *zeeskeit*. Bye!"

"Bye!" Zahava hung up the telephone and ran out the door.

Chezky charged into the kitchen just as the back door slammed. "Zahava!" he shouted. "Zahava, can I..." Too late, he thought. He slumped into a chair.

Ima's working is a pain in the neck! he thought. I want to go to Nachum's house and I have to tell someone and there's no one to ask. I can't go without telling and now I'm stuck. Chezky crossed his arms and stuck out his lower lip. They're all lucky that I'm such a good guy or I'd run off without telling anyone. When Ima was here, I didn't have these problems.

Suddenly, his eyes lit on the telephone. I know, I'll call Ima!

Chezky ran to the telephone and ran his finger down the list of telephone numbers. Carefully he dialed and waited.

"Hello, Sefer Press. May I help you?"

"I'd like to speak to my mother, uh, Mrs. Baker, please."

The voice on the telephone chuckled. "One moment, please. Shoshana, it's for you!"

Wow, thought Chezky, they don't call her Mrs. Baker.

"Hello?" came his mother's voice.

"Hi, Ima, it's Chezky! How are you?"

"*Baruch Hashem*, Chezky, I'm fine. What can I do for you? Is everything all right?"

"*Baruch Hashem*, fine, Ima. Was that your secretary? She didn't call you Mrs. Baker."

Mrs. Baker sighed. "She's the company's secretary and I went to school with her, so she knows me well and calls me by my first name. What can I do for you?"

"Can I go to Nachum's?" Chezky asked.

"That's why you called? Isn't there anyone there to ask? Where is everyone?"

"Well, Tikva and Rivka took Saraleh and Donny to the park. And Bracha is at the supermarket 'cause we ran out of something, I don't know what. And Moishy is working on his science project, and if I go near him he'll..."

"Never mind," Mrs. Baker cut in impatiently. "You may go, just leave a note."

"Thanks, Ima. Bye Ima!"

"Bye."

Chezky wrote a large note, posted it on the refrigerator, and left. The kitchen clock ticked and the refrigerator hummed. The kitchen door banged open and Yochie stalked into the room.

"That Moishy," she fumed. "I need that computer just as much as he does! I don't see why he has to have it all day and all night." She looked up to the ceiling. "Oh, I wish Ima was here!" Then she saw the telephone....

Moishy also saw the telephone and called his mother about his homework. Bracha was having trouble with dinner and thought her mother could help her, so she called, too.

The afternoon wore on. Zahava came back with her red thread. Chezky came home from his friend's. Gradually, the family congregated in the kitchen as dinner was prepared. At 5:30 everything was ready, but no Ima. Mr. Baker came home, but still no Ima.

"I think I'll call," said Mr. Baker, and he reached for the telephone. As he dialed, he said, "Quiet, please, everyone...quiet, please! I can't hear." A hush fell over the kitchen as they watched their father dial the number.

"Hello," said a tired voice. "Sefer Press, may I help you?"

"Hello, may I speak with Mrs. Baker, please?"

"One moment, please." He heard the secretary calling her name.

Mrs. Baker came on the line. In the silence of the

kitchen, the children could hear every word she said. "What is it now? I told you kids that I'm busy!"

Mr. Baker cleared his throat. "Nice secretary you got there."

There was a long silence. "Ephraim, I'm sorry. It's been a long day."

"So it has, " Mr. Baker replied. "When are you coming home?"

"Soon. You'd better start dinner without me."

"All right, but don't be long. Bye."

"Bye..." Mr. Baker hung up the telephone. He turned to the children and was greeted with a cacophony of complaints.

"Abba, we've had it!"

"Yes, we have. Ima can't miss dinner!"

"Things have gone too far!"

"I want Ima," Saraleh cried.

"Me, too!" shouted Donny.

"We're sick of life without Ima," said Yochie.

"We're sick of cold cereal in the morning, of peanut butter and jelly for lunch, and casserole for dinner," Moishy exclaimed.

"We're tired of spending our mornings running around like *mishugenas*, " added Zahava.

"And searching and searching through mountains of laundry for socks!" put in Chezky.

"And we're tired of babysitting for Saraleh!" Rivka glared at her little sister and folded her arms.

Saraleh began to cry. "I want Ima!"

Mr. Baker picked Saraleh up in his arms and

looked out at the sea of defiant faces. As the children read the disappointment in his expression, bit by bit their defiance melted.

"I guess things are very different around here..." he began.

"They are, Abba," said Tikva softly. "We really didn't want to complain, but it's been very hard. Really, it's been hard for you, too."

"I'm sorry I yelled," said Moishy. "I guess when you're used to things a certain way it's hard to get used to something different."

"Especially when things were that way because of Ima," said Dina.

"Maybe it's just all of the extra work," Bracha suggested. "Sometimes we don't feel like we have any time anymore. When I have to fix dinner, then all of the other things I have to do aren't fun because I have to rush, rush, rush."

"Yeah," Yochie agreed.

Mr. Baker looked at his children. Saraleh sniffed on his shoulder. "Okay, kids. I guess we'll have to come up with something. I'll talk it over with Ima, and I'm sure we'll come up with something."

They did talk. And talk. Until late that night, the light shone out from underneath Mr. and Mrs. Baker's door as they talked and telephoned and talked again. And as Moishy so clearly put it, the Baker kids realized that once again, something was up.

3
A Stranger Among Us

I can't look at this stuff," Bracha pushed her bowl of cold cereal away from her and put her head on the table.

"I know what you mean," said Moishy with his mouth full.

"No," said Bracha, her muffled voice coming out from under her arms. "That's not what I meant. I mean, I don't feel well. My stomach hurts."

"That's funny," Tikva began.

"I don't see anything funny about it," Bracha moaned.

"I meant that it was funny that you don't feel well," Tikva went on, "because I'm not feeling very well either."

"A stomachache?"

"No, my throat hurts." Tikva rubbed her neck.

"Your throat hurts?" asked Moishy. "I'll go and tell

Ima." He jumped up from the table and ran out of the room.

Bracha kept her head on the table. Tikva sat down next to her, leaned back, and closed her eyes.

"Do you feel sick enough to stay home?" she asked Bracha.

"I don't know," Bracha moaned. "Do you?"

"I don't know," Tikva answered. "Normally, I'd say yes, but I don't really want to stay home all alone, without Ima."

Bracha lifted up her head. "Wow, I'd forgotten that. Staying home alone, ugh." She put her head down again.

Mrs. Baker came into the kitchen. "What's going on here?" she asked.

"I have a stomachache," said Bracha.

"And my throat hurts," said Tikva.

"Hmmm, let me have a look at you." The girls stood up and Mrs. Baker examined both of them. "I guess you two better stay home today. *Refuah shelaimah.*" She looked up at the clock. "Oy, it's getting late. I've got to get the baby ready." She turned to go out of the kitchen.

Just then the doorbell rang.

"Who could that be at this hour?" Bracha wondered.

"The answer to all of our problems," said Mrs. Baker cryptically.

Donny burst into the kitchen. "Ima, Ima," he shouted. "There's some lady at the door and she wants you, I think, and I can't understand a word she says!"

"Coming!" Mrs. Baker and Donny went out of the kitchen. Tikva and Bracha looked at each other, mystified. Soon, Mrs. Baker was back, with most of the other Bakers and a strange woman.

The woman was short, in fact not much taller than Bracha. She had brown hair, lightly streaked with gray, and partially covered with a colorful scarf. When she smiled, the children could see two gold teeth. Over her slightly plump frame she wore an old, brown sweater and a nondescript polyester skirt. On top of that was a worn, checkered, wool coat. On her feet were black, lace-up shoes with short, chunky heels, and she carried a large, battered handbag.

"Children," said Mrs. Baker. "I'd like you to meet Zlata Rosenstein. She is going to be helping us out for a while."

"Hello," the woman smiled, her gold teeth sparkling.

"Hello," the children answered hesitatingly. Dina managed to choke out, "How do you do, Mrs. Rosenstein?"

"Mrs. Rosenstein is originally from Odessa, in Russia." Mrs. Baker continued, "She has been in America for two years. At night, she goes to school to learn English and Torah. During the day, she will work for us."

The children stared, open-mouthed.

"Please," said the woman in a heavy Russian accent. "Don't call me 'Mrs.' My name is Zlata."

Mrs. Baker introduced all of the children. "This is Bracha, our biggest girl. We have a bigger boy, Ashi. He is away at yeshiva; I hope you'll meet him soon. Next we have the quintuplets..."

"Qweentupplits?"

"Five born at the same time," Moishy informed her. "Quintuplets."

Zlata's eyes opened wide. "Ohhhhh," she said in wonder. "This is...special."

"Very special, *baruch Hashem*," agreed Mrs. Baker. "This is Rivka, Dina, Tikva, Yochie, and Zahava."

"Very nice," smiled Zlata.

"And here we have Moishy, Chezky, Donny, Saraleh and Rachel Ahuva."

"Very nice!" said Zlata. She scanned the rows of faces, stopping at Zahava. "You are Zahava, yes?"

"Yes," Zahava answered, wondering what she did to deserve special attention from this, well, strange woman.

"We have same name," Zlata smiled happily.

"What?" Zahava was appalled. She didn't want to have anything in common with this lady.

"Yes, is true," Zlata smiled again. "Zlata, Zahava, is same. Maybe you call me Zahava, too. I would like this; it is more Jewish." Zlata's gold teeth glittered.

Zahava opened her mouth, but no words came out. How could there be any comparison between her and this frumpy old Russian babushka!?

"Isn't that a nice idea," her mother was saying.

"We'd love to have another Zahava."

Zahava stared at her mother. Had she lost her mind?

"Yeah," Moishy was saying, "and sometimes, we can even call Zahava, Zlata." He looked at his sister with a mischievous gleam in his eye.

Zahava narrowed her eyes and glared at her brother. I'll talk to you later, she thought. Moishy stifled a giggle.

"Zlata, I mean, Zahava," said Mrs. Baker, "will be working for us most of the day. She'll be cooking, cleaning, folding the laundry — basically getting to everything that I don't have time for now that I'm working. I'm sure that she'll be wonderful adult company for all of you, too." Zlata nodded and smiled.

Dina cleared her throat. "Wonderful," she said wanly. Everyone stood around for an awkward moment. Then Zlata dug into her voluminous bag and took out an apron.

"Good," she said. "I now make breakfast...potatoes with butter is very good."

"Bracha, please show Zlata around the kitchen while I get the baby ready to go to Great-Aunt Frieda's." Mrs. Baker picked up the baby and started out of the kitchen. "The rest of you had better get ready for school now!"

The Baker children, galvanized into action, rushed out of the kitchen. Zahava dashed up the stairs two at a time, her head spinning. Ima going out to work was bad enough. This Russian lady was worse. Potatoes for breakfast! Who ever heard of such a thing?

"Zlata, darlink!" Zahava looked up. There, at the top of the stairs, was Moishy, his sweater wrapped around his head like a scarf.

"Moishy, I'll kill you!" Zahava charged up the rest of the stairs ready to throttle her brother. Moishy sprinted down the hall into his room and slammed the door.

"Zahava, calm down! It was only a joke." Dina was looking at her with disapproving eyes.

"Some joke," Zahava muttered. She pushed past Dina to her room.

In her room, Zahava went over to the mirror and began to fix her hair. Her sisters were talking about the new housekeeper.

"I never in a million years dreamed that Ima would hire someone to help us!" Yochie exclaimed as she pulled on her socks.

"Me neither!" Rivka agreed.

"You have to admit that it makes a lot of sense," said Tikva mildly. "We weren't managing, and this is going to give us all the breathing space we were asking for."

Yochie stamped her feet into her shoes. "But she looks so different. I never saw anyone with gold teeth before. I thought that people with gold teeth were only in books."

Tikva took up her brush and expertly ran it through her hair. "Did you expect someone from Russia to be the same as us?"

"I didn't expect someone from Russia," said Yochie as she joined her at the mirror.

"I understand that Russia is very behind the times with stuff like that," said Dina.

"I understand that they're behind the times with a lot of things," said Yochie with a sly look at Zahava. "Like with fashions." Zahava looked uncomfortable.

"Mmmm," Tikva agreed, with her barrettes in her mouth.

Yochie glanced quickly at her reflection and, satisfied, looked over at Zahava. A slow, naughty smile spread over her face. "She was so happy sharing a name with you, Zlata, oops, Zahava."

Zahava dropped what she was doing and hissed at her sister, "Don't call me that, ever!"

Yochie staggered back. "Okay, okay," she said. "Boy, what's your problem?"

"Seriously," said Tikva. "I think we should try to call her Zahava, if that's what she likes."

"I think you're right," Dina agreed.

"I don't," said Zahava through clenched teeth.

Bracha stuck her head in the door. "Ima's going soon, if you want to say good-bye," she said. "Aren't you staying home with me, Tikki?"

Tikva flopped on her bed. "I thought if I got going I might feel better, but it didn't work. I guess I'm staying home."

"Good," Bracha said. "I didn't feel like being alone. You can come into my room, and we can moan together."

"But Zlata's going to be here," put in Dina. "You

wouldn't have been alone."

"Hmmm," said Bracha noncommittally. "By the way, Ima said to tell you that Zlata is a 'Miss', not a 'Mrs.', so be extra-special nice to her." Bracha shook her finger at them and went out.

Zahava put the finishing touches on her outfit and turned to face her sisters. "Oh, Yochie!" she exclaimed.

"What?"

"Look what you're wearing!"

Yochie looked down at her plain uniform in bewilderment. "What's wrong?"

"Not the clothes," Zahava told her. "The sweater! That sweater is practically orange!"

"Is it?" Yochie looked at herself in the mirror. "So what?"

"Yochie, you can't wear an orange sweater!" Zahava was obviously upset.

"You can wear any color sweater with the uniform..."

"That's not the point," Zahava informed her. "That sweater is awful!"

Yochie began to feel annoyed. "I want you to know that Great-Aunt Freida gave this sweater to Cousin Brina, who gave it to me!"

"I can see why!" Zahava exclaimed. "She was probably thrilled that she could find someone to take it!"

"Zahava," Dina interrupted. "Don't you think you pick on Yochie too mcuh?"

"I'm not picking on her, I'm trying to help her," Zahava explained.

"Zahava, when I want your help, I'll ask for it. I'm running down to say good-bye to Ima," said Yochie. "I'm sorry you're not feeling well, Tikki, and Bracha too. *Refuah shelaimah*. Are you coming down?"

"No, I'll wave from the window."

"Feel better," Yochie told her. "Anyone else coming? How about you, Zahava, *darlink*?" She emphasized it with a fake Russian accent.

"No," Zahava said slowly. "I'll stay up here until it's time to leave for school."

"Okay!" she trilled. "*Dasvedanya!*" Yochie went out. The girls heard her thumping down the stairs.

"*Dasvedanya* is good-bye in Russian," Tikva translated. "I wonder where she picked that up?"

"Yochie is full of surprises," Rivka commented. "Feel better." She blew a kiss and went out.

"*Refuah shelaimah*," said Dina. "I'll go over the classwork with you when I get home."

"Thanks, Dini," Tikva waved.

Tikva and Zahava went over to the window, opened it wide, and leaned out. There was Ima, half in the car, buckling Rachel Ahuva into her car seat. When she finished, she looked up and they waved. She waved back. Then she waved to the other kids, got into the car, and drove off. Tikva and Zahava brought their heads back into the room and closed the window.

"Another day, another dollar," Tikva sighed.

"I guess so," Zahava sighed too.

"Somehow, today seems worse," Tikva commented.

"I know what you mean," said Zahava darkly.

"It would have been strange to stay home alone," Tikva said. "But it's stranger to stay home with a stranger."

"I don't envy you," Zahava told her.

"She seems like a nice woman," said Tikva, trying to look on the bright side. "And Bracha and I will get to know her faster than everyone else. That could be a help."

"I guess so...." Zahava stared glumly at her bed. I wish I could have stayed in there instead of waking up today, she thought. At least it's not raining.

"ZAHAVA!" her sisters shouted from downstairs. "It's time to go!"

Zahava dragged herself toward the bedroom door. "Good-bye Tikki, I hope you feel better," she said.

"Thank you, Zahava."

Zahava picked up her book bag and trailed through the Ima-less house to the kitchen, where her sisters were waiting.

"About time you got here," Yochie quipped.

"Good-bye girrrls," Zlata said. "You are lucky to go and study the Torah."

Zahava turned and studied the Russian woman. Her eyes traveled from her plain, black shoes to her old sweater to her round face, framed by her scarf and decorated by her gold teeth.

"Good-bye, Zahava," said Zlata. "It is good to share name, yes?"

Zahava was saved from answering by her sisters' insistent voices. She turned and fled the house.

4
Chezky's Diary #1

Testing, one, two, three! Testing, one, two, three! Is this thing working? (Click. Click.) Yes, it's working. Okay (ahem). The Diary of Yechezkel Baker, Chapter One.

Dear Diary. Hi, there.... Now what? (Click. Click.) Yochie said that I should write a diary. I said: No way! But Yochie thinks that it's time I tried to improve my mind, not just my curve ball. Dina said that Yochie should leave me alone, and Yochie told her to stay out of it. They started to have a fight, which was fine with me, because then I would be left alone. Then Tikva said that I didn't have to write; I could talk into a tape. No one had anything to say about that, so I said I'd think about it and went away, so no one could talk about it anymore.

Anyway, I thought about it. The more I thought about it the more I liked the idea. Everyone keeps diaries around here, so why not me? And talking into a tape is much better than writing. Easier too.

What can I tell you? Life here at the Bakers is upside down. Since Ima went to work, no one is normal anymore. I thought that her going to work sounded like a good idea. I mean, I miss her and all that stuff, but we needed the money and the job sounded like fun. It's got to be important stuff she's doing if there's a secretary.

All of the girls don't like what's happening at all. I guess that makes sense, because while life isn't all that different for me, they have to work harder. It's funny, though, that six girls can't replace one mother.

So we got this new helper who we just met. She's a Russian lady named Zlata, and she has two gold teeth. I wish I could look at them closer up, but I think Ima would tell me that it's impolite to ask. Maybe when we get to know her better.

Zahava almost hit the ceiling when Zlata said that her name was really Zahava, in Hebrew. It really bugs her. Zlata looks like a nice person. She has a Russian accent, so it isn't easy to understand her. I thought she said that she was making potatoes for breakfast!

I didn't say why Yochie thinks that I should improve my mind. There's going to be a Science Fair in school and she thinks it's about time that I did something for it. I told her that that's Moishy's department. She said, since when does Moishy have a monopoly on brains? (I didn't understand what a board game had to do with what we were talking about until she explained it to me.) Anyway, so she got me started on this diary. She calls it a journal. She said that all great scientists keep journals. I said maybe I'm not a great scientist. She told me to just be quiet and listen.

After Yochie decided that I was going to keep a diary and enter the Science Fair, she was nice enough to offer her help. When I said that maybe that wasn't fair, she said, "Ashi is helping Moishy, isn't he?"

So I guess it's fair.

So I said, "But Yochie, I don't even know what we should make."

So she said, "Don't worry, Chezky, I'll think of something."

So I said, "That's what I'm afraid of...."

"Chezky what are you doing? Do you know what time it is? You're not even half dressed! Turn that thing off!" (Click.)

5
Zahava on the Loose

A*pa-pa-las pteech-ka, stoy, Nye uy-dyosh eez sye-tee, Nye raz-ts-nem-sya sta-boy, Nee za shto na svyet-ye!"*

Bracha sat up in bed. "What's that?" she grimaced sleepily.

"What's what?" Tikva lifted her head off her pillow.

"That singing!" Bracha exclaimed.

Tikva lifted her head up higher and listened carefully.

"*Pteechka, pteechka!*" the voice warbled.

"It must be Zlata," Tikva decided, letting her head fall back onto her pillow.

"Zlata! I forgot about her." Bracha put her chin in her hands and sighed.

After everyone left, the two sick girls had gone upstairs and laid down in Bracha's room. The light was muted by the lowered shades and drawn curtains. The quiet in the almost-empty house made it easy for them to fall asleep. An hour or so later they woke to the sound of Zlata's singing.

"It sounds like a nice song," said Tikva.

"What does it mean?" Bracha wondered. "It sounds so mournful."

"We should ask."

Bracha's stomach growled. Tikva laughed. "I thought your stomach hurt!"

"It does," Bracha replied. "It's growling in pain."

"It sounds hungry to me."

"Well, maybe a little," Bracha admitted. "That sleep helped a lot."

"It helped me, too," Tikva said. She sat up and swung her legs over the bed. "Let's go and get some breakfast." The two girls put on robes and went down to the kitchen.

The singing got louder as they approached the kitchen. The song ended just as they opened the door. "*Ya na vyekee glaskee*." Zlata turned and smiled a broad smile at them. "So, good morrrrning!" she said cheerfully. "Are you feel better?"

"Yes, *baruch Hashem*," Tikva replied. "Thank-you."

"Yes, thank-you," Bracha echoed.

"Such good children, so polite," Zlata clasped her hands in admiration. "But you must be hungry?"

"Don't worry about us, Zlata," Tikva said quickly. "We'll help ourselves."

"No," said Zlata firmly. "Sick girls do not help. Sit!" She pointed to the chairs by the kitchen table. Unable to see a way out, the girls sat down and waited. Tikva noticed that her chair and the table were slightly damp.

From a huge pot on the stove, Zlata filled two bowls with boiled potatoes. She put them on the table along with butter, salt, and pepper. "This will be good," she said. "It will fill you up." She rubbed her stomach. "You start. I will make tea." She turned back to the counter.

Bracha and Tikva looked at each other and at the bowls, heaped high with steaming potatoes. Bracha swallowed hard.

"Dig in," said Tikva with an encouraging smile. She made a *berachah* and ate.

She had to admit that potatoes with butter were good, just not what she ever dreamed of eating for breakfast! She'd been thinking of tea and toast. Well, here is the tea anyway, she thought, as Zlata put hot cups of tea on the table.

"Is good?" Zlata asked.

"Yes, thank you," they answered.

"Good!" Zlata turned back to the counter.

Tikva blew on her tea to cool it. It looks dark, she thought. I guess they like it strong in Russia. She took a sip.

"Ugh," she said and quickly swallowed. She looked across at Bracha who was making a disgusted face.

Zlata hurried over looking worried. "Is no good?" she asked.

"No," Bracha replied in a hoarse voice, her eyes watering. "It's just a little hot."

"Yes," Tikva gasped. "Hot."

"Hot is good," said Zlata.

"Yes, fine," said Bracha. Satisfied, Zlata went back to the counter.

Tikva peered into the bottom of her cup. There was at least a quarter of an inch of sugar there! No wonder the tea was so sickly sweet! She scooped some sugar up with her spoon and watched it glide off in a syrupy stream. How many teaspoons could be in there? She saw Bracha queasily looking at hers.

"Uh, Zlata?" Zlata turned to them with her big smile. Tikva swallowed nervously. "Uh, Zlata? We found out that we don't feel as good as we thought." Bracha nodded in agreement. "We're going to lie down for a while." Bracha nodded again.

"Oish," Zlata put both hands on her cheeks and shook her head in concern. "This is no good. Big girls should feel good." Then she saw the almost full cups of tea. "T-t-t-t-t-t-t-t-t-t-t-t!" she said with her tongue. "You must drink! Sick people must drink!"

The two girls looked at each other. What now?

"I think I want a cold drink, Zlata," Bracha said quickly. She started to get up from her chair.

"No good," Zlata shook her head. "Cold not good for sick people." She pointed to the cups of tea on the table and crossed her arms. "Drink. Your mother — your Ima — said I am to take care of you."

Bracha sat back down and looked at Tikva. Bravely,

Tikva picked up her cup and drank. She managed to drain most of the cup in one try. Bracha looked at her cup, down into its dark, brown, syrupy depths, and closed her eyes. She took one sip. The tea, now luke-warm, tasted worse than ever. Suddenly, she had an idea.

"Zlata, I'm going to take this to my room and drink the rest in bed." She stood up quickly and picked up the cup.

"Okay, that is good," Zlata said cheerfully. "Feel better. How do you say it? *Refuah shelaimah!*"

"Thank you, Zlata, see you later," Bracha said as casually as she could. Before Zlata could say anything else, they fled the kitchen.

They didn't speak until they reached Bracha's room. Then Tikva flung herself on the bed and moaned.

"Uuuuuuuuuuuuuungh....Now I feel nauseous!"

"You poor thing!" Bracha said sympathetically. "I don't know how you drank it!"

"I wish I'd thought of your idea; I'll never be the same again!" Tikva clutched her stomach dramatically.

"Seriously, Tikki, that was really a mitzvah of *ve'ahavtah le'rayecha kamocha.* I'm sure her feelings would have been hurt."

"Mmmmmmmmmmugh," Tikva groaned. "What are you going to do with your tea?"

"I guess I'll put it down the bathroom sink," Bracha sighed. "Do you suppose it's safe?"

"What do you mean?"

"I mean, what if it plugs up the drain or corrodes the pipes or something."

"Ooooooh! My poor stomach!" Tikva cried. The girls broke into paroxysms of laughter.

After they stopped laughing, Bracha tiptoed down the hall and into the bathroom. Carefully she poured the syrupy liquid down the drain. The little that spilled on the sink made a dark mark that she rubbed off with a piece of tissue. After she rinsed the sink, she snuck down the hall again, sliding through the door of her room and closing it quickly behind her. She leaned against it, panting.

"What's wrong?" Tikva asked.

"Quick," Bracha gasped. "Call a plumber!" Tikva laughed and threw a pillow at her.

They went into the quints' room and borrowed all of the pillows. With pillows piled high, they settled themselves into the beds in Bracha's room and read. From the window, a rectangle of light moved slowly across the floor, lighting up the dancing dust motes in its path. The sounds and smells of home surrounded the girls in a quilt of comfort and well-being.

Bracha was reading *Faithful Soldiers*. She'd taken a package of tissues into bed with her and had already used them all up. Now she sat straight up in bed; six men had just come to get Yankele! How was he going to get out of this one?

"*Pteechka, pteechka! Kak lyoobeet Mi tyebya bi stalee...*"

"What's that?" Tikva asked.

"It's just Zlata," Bracha shushed her with an impatient gesture.

"No, not the singing," Tikva said. "I smell ammonia, and there's running water somewhere!"

Bracha looked up from her book. There was a powerful smell in the air, and it sounded as if gallons of water were being splashed everywhere. "Do you think it's Zlata?" she asked.

"Who else could it be? But why does it smell so bad?"

"Maybe something spilled," Bracha guessed.

"Maybe..." said Tikva thoughtfully. "We'd better check it out."

Bracha sighed and closed her book. Both girls donned slippers and went in search of Zlata.

They found her in Saraleh's room. The windows were wide open and the rug was rolled back. The bed was stripped and all of Saraleh's beloved toys and dolls were dumped on top of it. Zlata was washing the window. Next to her was a huge basin of water, reeking of ammonia. There was water everywhere. Bracha clapped her hand over her nose and looked around her in horror.

"*A pa-pa-las pteeech-ka, stoy...*" Zlata warbled. She stopped what she was doing when she noticed the girls and smiled at them. "Hello! Do you feel better?" she asked.

"A little," Tikva coughed.

Zlata shook her head. "It does not sound too much better..."

"No, really, it's fine. I mean, I'm fine," Tikva protested. She backed out of the room, Bracha behind her. The two girls stood out in the hall listening, as Zlata resumed her cleaning and her song.

"Different cleaning methods," Bracha said at last.

"Unique," Tikva agreed.

"I think I'll go downstairs." Bracha got her book and went downstairs. Not long afterwards, Tikva joined her.

"She's doing your room," she told Bracha.

"Oh." Bracha gestured to the window seat where she was sitting. "Make yourself at home. I was just about to get a drink. Want one?"

"Yes, please," Tikva replied. "But not tea!"

Bracha gave her a wry grin, put her book down in a corner of the window seat, and went to the kitchen.

It certainly looks sparkling clean in here, she thought. She noticed that the windows were wide open despite the fact it was a chilly day. I guess that's a good idea if no one's in here. It will certainly help to get rid of the smell of ammonia! She poured two cups of orange juice and went back to Tikva. After sitting down, she made a *berachah*, drank, and picked up her book.

"It's wet!" she exclaimed.

"Orange juice usually is," Tikva said without looking up.

"I meant my book is wet. It's sopping wet!" Bracha held up the dripping book. "And look here under the cushions! The whole window seat is still wet."

Tikva picked up a cushion and looked at the wet patch underneath.

As they stared at the ruined book, Zlata came singing down the stairs. "*Pteechka, pteeechka,*" she sang as she burst into the room. "Hello!" she smiled at them pleasantly. She bent down and picked up a rag that was on the floor. "I forget this. Feeling better?"

Bracha looked at Zlata, then at her sopping wet book and at the soaked window seat, and made a snap decision. "Yes, I'm feeling much better," she said quickly. "I think I'll call my mother and go to school."

Zlata looked worried. "This is sure?" she asked. "Maybe you should stay home. Rest and drink tea."

"No, no, Zlata, it's okay!" Bracha said frantically. "I'm fine! I hate to miss school!" Please, she thought no more tea!

"Okay, but..." Zlata began.

"Come, Tikki, let's go and call now, during Ima's coffee break." She dragged Tikva out of the room and down the hall to the study.

"Bracha," Tikva whispered fiercely, "are you out of your mind?"

"I don't know about you," Bracha hissed back, "but I don't want to stay around here any more. Just the smell of the ammonia could send me running out of the house."

Tikva sniffed. "I know what you mean," she said. "But what was that about Ima's coffee break?"

"Look," Bracha said, her cheeks a little flushed. "I

know Ima takes a coffee break. I don't know exactly when, but I had to get out of there. Did you want another cup of tea?"

Tikva clutched at her stomach and shook her head. Point made, Bracha went to the telephone and dialed.

"But, Bracha," Tikva objected, "Ima will be furious. We said we were sick and now we want to go to school. I don't think she'll like that! And she doesn't want us to call her at work unless it's an emergency."

"For me," Bracha stated, "this is an emergency!" Tikva put her head next to Bracha's so she could hear the telephone conversation.

"Hello! Sefer Press, may I help you?"

"May I speak with Mrs. Baker please?" Bracha asked.

"Who shall I say is calling?"

Bracha gulped. She hadn't expected this question! What if Ima wouldn't talk to her? "Bracha Baker, uh, her daughter."

"One moment, please." Bracha heard a muffled conversation in the background. "Excuse me," the secretary came on the line again. She sounded amused. "Mrs. Baker would like to know if this is an emergency, and if so, on a scale of one to ten where does it rate?"

An emergency? On a scale of one to ten? I just want to talk to my mother! "It's not an emergency, but I'd like to talk to her. It's pretty important." She heard another muffled conversation and her mother came on the phone.

"Hello?"

"Oh, Ima. I'm sorry to bother you..."

"It's okay, Bracha, just make it quick."

"Ima, Tikki and I are feeling better and we want to go to school." Bracha winced, waiting for the explosion. Before it came, she could hear someone calling her mother.

"Just a minute, I'm coming! Are you sure?"

"Huh?"

"Bracha, are you sure you're feeling better?" her mother asked.

"Yes, *baruch Hashem*." Oh, I hope she says yes, Bracha thought anxiously.

"All right, then go. Tell your teachers that I'll send a note tomorrow. Bye-bye *zeeskeit*, I gotta run. I love you!"

"I love you too..." Bracha started to say, but her mother had already hung up. Bracha roughly hung up the telephone. "Let's get dressed and get out of here," she growled.

As they got ready, she fumed to Tikva, "Imagine having to apologize for wanting to talk to my own mother! Imagine having to talk to a secretary first!" Tikva didn't disagree.

"We'd better tell Zlata that we're going," said Tikva.

"You're right," Bracha confirmed. They located her in Moishy's room by the sound of her voice.

"*Pteechka, pteechka*," she was singing. She turned to the girls as they came into the room. "Hello!" she sang.

"Hello," they answered uncertainly.

"I see you are going to school. Very good!"

"Yes, " said Bracha. "We just wanted to say good-bye." She wondered how you say good-bye after such a big hello.

"Good-bye!" said Zlata. She waved enthusiastically.

"Good-bye," the girls waved back uncomfortably. After an awkward pause they left the room, gathered their things, and left the house.

"Did you look at Moishy's room?" Bracha asked Tikva as they walked along. "I don't think he's going to be too happy."

"What do you mean?" Tikva asked.

"What I mean is," said Bracha, "that things looked, well, rearranged."

Tikva sighed. "I'll bet that's not the only place."

After the sensation of two of the Baker girls coming in late, school settled into it's usual routine. The chilly walk home in the late afternoon sunshine was invigorating, but did not help prepare them for what had happened in their absence.

As Bracha walked past Saraleh's room, she heard a soft sobbing. Opening the door, she found Saraleh sitting on the floor staring at her toys, tears streaming down her face. The room still smelled of ammonia.

Bracha went to her and took her in her arms. "Saraleh, what's wrong?" she asked.

"My-my-my toooys!" Saraleh buried her head in Bracha's hair and cried.

Bracha looked at Saraleh's toy shelves. The shelves gleamed. Her host of dolls were primly sitting, arranged in order of size. Her doll house, sparkling clean, had been moved into a corner, and all of the furniture was placed neatly in a box in the living room. The doll clothes were nowhere to be seen. Things were not as Saraleh had left them that morning.

Bracha felt for her little sister. Her dolls were her treasures. She spent hours dressing and arranging them and knew just how she liked them. She knew which doll was whose baby and which were her own babies and which dolls liked to sit together. Her doll house was a masterpiece, each piece of furniture painstakingly placed in just the right spot. When Saraleh walked into her room this afternoon it must have been like walking into the room of a stranger!

"Shh, Saraleh, shhh," Bracha comforted her. "I'll help you fix it, don't cry."

Yochie stuck her head into the room. "Bracha! You'll never believe..." she began. Then she saw Saraleh in Bracha's arms with tears running down her face. "What's going on here?" she asked.

"I guess when Zlata cleaned in here she rearranged the toys a little," Bracha explained. "Saraleh feels like everything is ruined. But we're going to fix everything up, aren't we, Saraleh darling?"

Saraleh sniffed and nodded.

"Here too?" Yochie squeaked. "I just spent goodness-knows-how-long helping Chezky fix up his army base. Zlata took it apart when she cleaned his room.

Do you want me to help here, too?"

Bracha and Saraleh were grateful for Yochie's help. Better than Bracha, she remembered which dolls sat where and what they wore. She cheered Saraleh up by playing "moving man" when they set up the doll house. There was a worrisome moment when they couldn't find the doll clothes, until Yochie thought of looking in Rachel Ahuva's clothes.

"I don't believe this," Bracha said as they came across the doll clothes, neatly folded, among Rachel Ahuva's things.

"This would never happen if Ima was around," Yochie said firmly.

"Never!" Saraleh echoed.

Just as they finished, they heard a yell from down the hall.

"That sounds like Moishy," said Yochie.

Bracha, remembering what she saw that morning, ran down the hall to Moishy's room, Yochie and Saraleh right behind her. There was Moishy, staring into the box where he was supposed to keep his Lego collection. He rarely kept it there because it was almost always tied up in some project or another. In the box, neatly sorted, each kind of piece in its own compartment, was Moishy's entire Lego collection. The girls gaped in amazement.

"Did you do that?" Yochie asked.

"Are you kidding me?" Moishy cried. "I was in the middle of a major project. I was making a space shuttle and mission control. I left it on the floor this morning because I knew I'd be coming back to it right after school, and now look." He thrust the box under their noses. "How did this happen?"

Yochie looked around the room mysteriously and sniffed. The air smelt faintly of ammonia. "Zlata strikes again," she announced.

"How did she find the time?" Bracha was amazed. "She must be an incredibly fast worker!"

"Ima would never do this," Moishy muttered.

"Never!" Saraleh echoed. As they stood and stared at the box in commiseration with Moishy, another commotion was heard down the hall.

"What is it now?" Yochie wailed. She ran out of the door followed by the others.

This time it was Donny. They found him surrounded by the rest of the family, his face flushed in anger.

"I put my wallet under my pillow this morning," he was saying. "It was full of money! I went to get it, and it was gone!" Donny crossed his arms and glared at the sea of faces.

"Wait!" Yochie cried. "We must investigate." She peered around the room. "Notice: The bed is made. The windows are gleaming. The shelves are shining." She sniffed. "There is a smell of ammonia in the air," she whispered. "It can only be one thing! Only one person could have done this!" She paused dramatically and raised one finger. "Zlata strikes again!"

"She wants to be called Zahava," commented Dina.

"Oh, no, you don't," Zahava shook her finger at Dina.

"That's beside the point!" Yochie cried.

"If she wants to be called Zahava, I don't see why..."

"Silence!" Yochie jumped on a chair. "We must organize a search! Everyone fan out. The first person to find the wallet..."

"There can't be a first person to find the wallet, Yochie," Moishy interrupted. "It can only be found once."

"SILENCE!" Yochie roared. "When the wallet is found, the person who finds it should run to the top of the stairs and shout: 'I found it.' Any questions?"

"Who put you in charge?" Rivka asked.

"Irrelevant!" Yochie proclaimed. "Everyone ready? One, two, three..."

"Hello!" There was Zlata smiling from ear to ear.

"Hello," the children responded in a ragged chorus.

Zlata smiled some more. "It is nice to see so many good children together," she said.

"Uh, yes," said Bracha.

"What is the game?"

It took the children a moment to realize that she was asking what they were playing. "Um, Hide and Go Seek," said Yochie quickly.

"Very nice," said Zlata. "Soon is supper, okay?"

"Okay," said Yochie.

"Very nice," said Moishy. Rivka kicked him with the side of her shoe. Zlata smiled and left the room.

"She has shiny teeth, like Ima's ring," Saraleh said.

"Attention," Yochie cried. "Once again: One, two three, go!" She leapt off of the chair and out of the room.

Dina and Rivka decided to search Donny's room. To them it made the most sense that the wallet was still there. Zahava took the homework room. Tikva and Yochie decided that since they'd been lucky there before, they would look through the baby's things. Donny and Saraleh looked in the bathroom. Moishy, after some thought, went into his room and looked under Ashi's pillow. There was the wallet! He rushed to the top of the stairs and shouted, "I found it!" The other children came running.

"Oh, Moishy, thank you, thank you!" Donny was dancing with joy.

"Where did you find it?" Bracha asked.

"Under Ashi's pillow," Moishy replied.

"Under Ashi's pillow?" Yochie squeaked. "What made you think to look there?"

"Elementary, my dear Yochie," said Moishy. "Donny is the youngest boy, Ashi is the oldest. Simple deductive logic."

Yochie couldn't think of a thing to say.

6
Chezky's Diary #2

(Click. Click.)

"Oops! (Click. Click.) Okay, here we go.

The Diary of Yechezkel Baker, Chapter Two. (Cough, cough.)

I'm beginning to think this diary business isn't so bad after all. For example, when you've got things on your mind, it's a good place to get them all straight. Tikva says she does it all the time with her diary. So here goes.

If I was writing this I'd make an outline, like we do in school, because Yochie says it's more scientific. Since I'm just talking, I'll say it in numbers.

1: Ima is never around. I know I complained about this before, but it's gotten worse.

2: Zlata/Zahava. She's a nice lady, but she turns the house upside-down whenever she cleans. Also, she keeps serving potatoes. She makes them creamed, mashed, boiled, baked, with butter, with sour cream, with gravy, with oil, with borscht (ugh and yuk), I can't go on. Now, I like potatoes as much as anyone, but enough is enough. (Bracha says that it's not her fault, almost the only thing they had to eat in Russia was potatoes.)

3: Zahava. My sister, that is. First of all, she hits the ceiling whenever anyone calls Zlata, Zahava. And she can't take a joke. The other day I asked her to help me out with something, and I talked in this fake Russian accent. I thought she was going to hit me or something.

Second of all, since she joined the Sewing Club she's been driving us all crazy. She doesn't like the way anyone dresses, especially me and Yochie. And she wants to redecorate the house. She wanted to put up red curtains with teddy bears in my room, for crying out loud!

4: Ima is never home. That's so lousy, I get to say it twice.

There is a bright spot, something really good. Do you remember the reason I started this diary in the first place? Because Yochie said I had to improve my mind and that the way to do that was to do a project for the Science Fair? Well, she has an idea, a really great idea. What we're going to do is...

"Chezky, BEDTIME!" (Click.)

7
Zahava vs. Zahava

teechka, pteechka."

Zahava buried her head in her hands. "There she goes again," she moaned. "Doesn't she know another song?"

The Baker girls were in the homework room, doing homework and catching up on various projects. Tikva sat at the computer, typing a report. Bracha was playing soft tunes on the piano. Dina, Rivka, Yochie, and Zahava were sitting at the long table, surrounded by books, book bags, pencils, and notebooks. Through the door, they could hear Zlata bustling up and down the hall, doing housework.

"I've heard her singing other things," Dina informed her. "But this one is one of her favorites."

"If I hear it one more time I might go out of my mind," Zahava declared.

"Oh?" Yochie said archly, "do you have a m..."

"What is a '*pteechka*' anyway?" Rivka interrupted diplomatically.

"It's a bird. Like a '*tzipor*' in Hebrew," Tikva informed them. "The song is about a bird that is caught by a small boy. The boy wants to keep the bird and offers it sweet things and candy. The bird only wants to be free and explains to the boy that sweets will only make it sick and die."

"What a sad song!" Yochie declared.

"I guess so," said Tikva thoughtfully. "Zlata says it's a little like the story of the Jews in other countries. The goyim say that they'll give us sweet things, like their religions or philosophies, but that's really poison to us. We don't need their sweets, we need to be free to serve Hashem."

"Wow," said Rivka. "I didn't know that Zlata said things like that."

"You should talk to her more," Tikva told her.

"All Zlatas should be talked to more," Yochie said in a Russian accent. She turned to Zahava. "Isn't that right, darlink? How's the potato business?"

Zahava glared at her, eyes blazing.

"Don't mention potatoes!" Tikva moaned, diverting another run-in between Yochie and Zahava.

Zahava, struggling for self-control, turned back to her notebook. They all think they're so funny, she fumed to herself. Well, I have more important things to do than sit and listen to them....

Zahava thought back to that afternoon's Sewing Club meeting. The lampshades were a good idea; each person's lampshade was beautiful and really unique. It was a nice feeling to know that all over Bloomfield there were beautiful lampshades hanging, thanks to the B.Y. of Bloomfield Sewing Club.

Shani Roberts came up with the idea of starting a scrapbook. Each lampshade was photographed. (Zahava took her picture with Rachel Ahuva under the lampshade. It was so cute!) Then all of the pictures were labeled and put into an album. The album was arranged so that there was a page of pictures, then a page of instructions, then a page of pictures again. Now, future B.Y. Sewing Clubs would have a book of ideas to use and add to.

After they'd finished the album, they talked about new project ideas. Different ideas were discussed, but nothing was agreed on.

"Listen," said Devoiry Schorr. "We're not getting anywhere this way. I think that we should take turns — each member should think of a project for the whole club."

"What a great idea!" said Fraidie Glass, the club leader. Turning to Zahava, she said, "Zahava you're one of the best sewers here and you always have great ideas. You can be first!"

Zahava accepted enthusiastically. They decided that she would come to the next meeting with her idea already planned out so they could start on it right away. The meeting broke up with much excited talk.

On the way home, Zahava had found her enthusiasm waning. How in the world was she going to figure out a project for all of those girls? They were all on different levels of skill; some could hardly sew at all. How could she think of something that would get everyone involved?

"Zahava, what's on your mind?" Rivka asked. "You've hardly said a word since you got home."

"I'm thinking about sewing projects," Zahava sighed. "For the club. I wish we could redesign the uniform..."

"Oh, you and that uniform!" Yochie exclaimed. "What is so awful about the uniform?"

Zahava stared down her nose at Yochie. "*Vehameivin yavin,*" she said.

"What?" Yochie asked.

"He who is able to understand, will understand," Tikva said absently, her thoughts on her computer.

"What is it that I'm supposed to be understanding," Yochie asked, her voice tense. "Or not understanding, as the case may be?"

"It's not as if we haven't talked about this before," Zahava began.

"It certainly isn't," muttered Rivka.

"Darlink," said Yochie in her Russian accent. "First, the prrrrrrroblem is the colors, da? Is this not so...Zlata, oops, I mean, Zahava? It would be better to see in basic brown, maybe?"

"Yochie," Rivka warned her.

Zahava decided to change her tactics. "Look," she said. "We all agree that a Jewish woman has to dress nicely, that a person is *betzelem Elokim* and has to take care of herself, right?"

The other girls agreed.

"Every time the girls of Bais Yaakov walk down the street it should be a *kiddush Hashem*, right?"

Everyone agreed.

"So we do have to think about our appearances," Zahava continued. "Now if you walk down the street in something hopelessly out-of-date..."

"That's where we begin to go wrong," Tikva commented.

"What do you mean?"

"She means that you have to be careful about that kind of thing," Dina interjected.

"It's okay to keep up with the fashions to a point," Tikva continued.

"I don't see what you're driving at," Zahava said.

"Well," Tikva said, "for example, short skirts are very 'in' now."

Zahava was shocked. "Who ever said anything about short skirts?"

"Just talking about how one thing can lead to another," Tikva said, turning back to her computer.

How did we get to talking about short skirts? Zahava wondered to herself. She decided to try again.

"Never mind Bais Yaakov," she said. "Let's just look at the Bakers."

"Let's not and say we did," Yochie quipped.

"Each person could do so many little things to improve her appearance," Zahava went on. "Take Dini's hair."

"I don't want to take Dini's hair," said Yochie. "I've got my own. Besides, Dini would look silly without her hair."

"Yochie," Bracha warned her.

"One minute she's talking about being a *kiddush Hashem* in the street, the next, she wants to shave Dini's head." Yochie was indignant. "It must be all of that communist indoctrination"

"What are you talking about?" Zahava demanded.

"Russia isn't a communist state anymore," Tikva reminded them.

"Darlink!" Yochie added with an exaggerated big grin. They all wrote for a few minutes in silence. Suddenly, Yochie asked, "Why don't you make kites?"

"Kites? Kites are made out of paper!"

"Not all kites," Yochie informed her. "The fancy ones are made out of cloth. This is just the right kind of weather for them."

"Actually," said Tikva, "It's too windy for kites. You need a breeze, not a strong wind. A very strong wind blows them apart."

"Oh," said Yochie, "I didn't know that."

"I don't know why I bother talking to you people about this sort of stuff." Zahava slumped back in her chair and crossed her arms.

"Me neither," Rivka muttered.

Just then, Moishy burst into the homework room. He ran over to the piano and played "ta-dah!" very loud. "I did it!" he sang.

"You did what?" Yochie asked.

"I foiled Zahava!" he said triumphantly.

"You foiled me?" Zahava asked.

"Not you," said Moishy, "Zlata/Zahava."

"Will you stop..." Zahava began.

"What did you do?" Yochie asked.

"I put all of my Lego in the attic," he informed them. "She'll never find it there!"

"Don't be too sure," Rivka muttered darkly.

"Yeah," Yochie agreed. "Never underestimate the power of a Zlata." She turned to Zahava. "Isn't that true, Zlata, darlink?"

"If you don't..." Zahava sputtered.

"It's true," said Moishy thoughtfully. "Not everyone could think of a thousand-and-one ways to make potatoes. Isn't that so, Zlata, darlink?"

"Or a thousand-and-one ways to use ammonia," Rivka added. "Right, Zlata, oops, I mean Zahava?"

"I don't have to stay here and take this," Zahava cried, standing up suddenly and knocking over her chair.

"*Dasvedanya*," Moishy and Yochie waved and collapsed in paroxysms of laughter. Zahava stomped out of the room.

"*Dasvedanya*?" Dini asked.

"See ya' later," Moishy informed her. "In Russian."

Zahava stormed down the hall. Everyone here is driving me out of my mind, she thought. How can so many people be so obtuse?

She went to her room and flopped down on her bed. And I still haven't thought of a project, she frowned. She lay down and stared at the ceiling. Well, sitting here doing nothing isn't going to help. I'd better finish my homework. Oh, my books are in the homework room. She got up and went back down the hall.

"Zlata, oops, I mean, Zahava, darlink!" Yochie greeted her. She rolled her eyes to the ceiling. "I always get those two mixed up!" she said, snapping her fingers.

"One potato, two potato, three potato, four..." Moishy chanted.

Zahava charged past them, stuffed all of her books into her book bag and ran out, slamming the door behind her.

She finished her homework and looked around for something to do. I am not going back into that homework room, she thought. That is for sure.

Her eyes lit on her closet. Ah! she thought. Today would be the perfect day to rearrange my closet.

She hauled everything out of her closet — skirts, dresses, blouses, shoes — and dumped them on her bed. I should have done this a long time ago, she thought. Look at this blouse. It's too small for me, but I bet it will still fit Yochie. She threw the blouse onto Yochie's bed. I never wear this shirt. Wow, this shirt goes perfectly with my plaid skirt; I never thought of that!

Zahava worked steadily for an hour and then stood back to admire her handiwork. The clothing was arranged in order, each outfit on its own hanger. Her school clothes were on the left, then regular clothes, then clothes that were a little bit dressy, and then Shabbos clothes. The dress that she wore to her cousin's wedding was last of all. On the floor underneath were her shoes, neatly lined up from her sneakers to her patent leathers.

"That is a job well done," she said, dusting off her hands.

The door banged open and Yochie leapt into the room.

"Can't you just walk into a room?" Zahava asked her.

Yochie turned around and walked out. Then she quietly walked back in again. "Yes," she replied. "I can. I wasn't sure, so I figured I'd better try it before I answered you." She noticed the open closet door and the row of clothes and shoes. "Zahava, darlink, you've been at it again!" She clasped her hands together and rocked from side to side. "It is so beeeyoootiful!" She sniffed the air and feigned disappointment. "But there is no ammonia!" she cried.

"Ha," Zahava said. "Ha,ha,ha." She went over to Yochie's bed. "Look, I have a blouse for you. It was one of my favorites, but it's too small. I think it will still fit you."

"Ooo-oo-oo! A blouse for little, old, frumpy Yochie!"

"Never mind," said Zahava in disgust, snatching the blouse from her sister.

Yochie realized that she went too far. "No, seriously," she said, "it's a nice blouse and I'd be glad to have it."

Zahava considered.

"Really," Yochie coaxed her. "I'm sorry if I acted like I didn't want it."

Slowly, Zahava handed the blouse to her.

"Thanks," Yochie said and stuffed the blouse into her drawer. Zahava winced.

"Well, I'll see you soon," Yochie said as she went out. "It's almost potato time."

All that night and the next day, Zahava thought and worried about her sewing project. She had to come up with something before the next meeting, and she still couldn't think what!

She tried discussing it with her mother in the evening. Before she got very far, the telephone rang and she was unavailable again. The next morning she didn't have any time, of course. It didn't help that her brothers and sisters were on the warpath, continuously teasing her about Zlata/Zahava. I don't know how anyone can think creatively in this kind of atmosphere, she thought bitterly.

The next day, Tuesday, was no better. She came home and found a bag on her bed with a potato in it. It had a card inside that said: "With love from all of us." But the worst was yet to come.

As she was doing her homework, she noticed a loose button on her blouse. I'll sew that on before it falls off so I don't lose it, she thought. Just as soon as I finish my homework.

Just as she was finishing her last math problem, Chezky burst into the homework room. "You gotta see this," he yelled, and was out of the room before anyone could ask him what it was that they had to see. They all ran after him and followed him to his room. They found him in front of his closet. "Look!" he cried, and flung open the door.

Instead of the usual jumble of clothes, books, and toys, there was complete order. His shirts and pants hung in neat rows. His shoes, neatly sorted into pairs, were in his shoe bag. Some of the toys were in boxes, while others were on shelves with the books. The books were lined up in order of size. There was a faint odor of ammonia.

"I didn't believe it could be done," said Dina slowly.

"Don't touch it!" Rivka cried. "Ever!"

"Wait!" Yochie ran out of the room. She came back with a camera. "Stand in front of the open door, Chezky. We'll take a picture to remember this forever."

Chezky posed, the camera flashed. They all took one last look at the immaculate closet. "Zlata strikes again," said Yochie reverently. Chezky closed the closet door and bowed.

That was amazing, Zahava thought as she went down the hall to her room. I'm glad that no one would ever have to do that to my closet, she thought smugly, as she pictured in her mind the sorted and hanging clothes above the neat row of shoes in her closet. Well, I'd better change my blouse so I can sew that loose button. She went to her closet and opened the door. As she looked through her clothes, she began to realize that something was wrong.

Where is my beige blouse? she thought, panic rising. Why can't I find it? What's going on here? She looked down and saw that her shoes were in the wrong order. Whose been playing around in here? Then she smelled a faint odor of ammonia.

"Hello!" said a voice. Zahava spun around. It was Zlata!

"You!" she gasped.

Zlata was smiling from ear to ear. "Today I did the closet. All of the closets," she informed her. "It's nice, yes?"

"Oh, very nice!" Zahava brushed past her and ran out of the house.

Zahava plowed down the street; she was so upset she could hardly see. I can't believe this is happening, she said to herself, I just can't believe this is happening!

All this is because Ima is out working. Everything is upside down; everything is crazy. Since when does anyone touch my closet, my things? I take care of my things and no one needs to touch them. That crazy Russian lady ruined everything!

I don't know why Ima and Abba hired her; she doesn't know what she's doing. The house is a disaster. You can't find a thing. We eat potatoes morning, noon, and night. The only thing we haven't had is potato sandwiches, and I'm waiting for them!

Zahava sat down on a bench and glared at the traffic. The people drove by, indifferent to her plight.

Well, this is it, she thought angrily. I've had it! If no one else in the family is willing to do anything about this, then I'll do it myself. Things have got to get better — they couldn't be any worse.

That night, after supper, Zahava tapped on the door of her father's study.

"Come in," her father called out in his warm, cheerful voice. Zahava let herself in and closed the door. She loved her father's study. It reminded her of her father: warm, cheerful, and full of Torah!

"Hello!" said Mr. Baker. "What can I do for you Zahavaleh? You look a little down in the mouth."

"Oh, Abba," Zahava began.

"That bad, huh?" Mr. Baker asked sympathetically.

"Oh, Abba, listen." Zahava sat down and leaned forward. "Abba, we've all been trying really hard since Ima went to work, but it just isn't working; nothing is the same. Zlata is probably a nice lady, I mean, she is a nice lady, but...well, she doesn't do things like Ima. We eat potatoes all the time, she rearranges everything, and everything smells like ammonia. Today she went through all my stuff. You know how neat I keep my stuff — Ima never needs to clean up my stuff. Abba, we've had it. We want Ima back."

"Did you talk to the other kids before coming to me? Did they know you were coming to tell me all this?" her father asked her.

"Well," Zahava answered uneasily, "no, I didn't. But I know everyone agrees with me."

"Hmmm." Mr. Baker closed his eyes and thought for a moment. Then he opened them and looked straight at Zahava. "It must have been very upsetting for you to come home and find all of your things mixed up," he said.

"It sure was!" Zahava agreed vehemently.

"I'll talk to Zlata about touching your things."

"Thank-you Abba," Zahava said, "but what about everything else?"

Mr. Baker sighed. "I have to admit, we knew Ima's new job would be time consuming, but we didn't realize just how much time it would consume. But," he added, raising one finger, "this is only the beginning. Once things are established there, she won't have to work as hard. All beginnings are difficult, Zahava. Things will get better later on. It won't be like this forever."

Zahava looked at her father. At first, she had felt better knowing that he understood, but now she saw that nothing would really change. *I'll just have to grin and bear it somehow,* she thought. *I hope Abba's right. I don't want it to be like this forever.*

"Okay?" her father asked her. His smile was kind and understanding.

"Okay, Abba." Zahava kissed her father and went out.

Later that night, Zahava passed the study again. The light was on and her father was on the telephone. She stopped to tie her shoe and, without intending, heard part of his telephone conversation.

"So what time do you think you'll be home?" He could only be speaking to Ima. "Hmm...okay sweetheart, I'll see you then. We're behind you, Shoshana. Good-bye." Mr. Baker hung up the telephone.

Zahava peeked through the door. Her father was sitting back in his chair, staring at the ceiling. His fingers went tap, tap, tap, on one arm of his chair.

Abba looks worried, she thought. He looks worried and he looks...lonely. Usually at night, her parents spent at least an hour talking, catching up on the day's events and whatever else they talked about. How did it feel to Abba to come home to a tired Ima, or to no Ima when she worked late? He must miss her, too!

Zahava thought that maybe she should knock on the door, just to go into the study and say hello, but something held her back. With a sigh, she moved away from the study door and made her way to her room.

8
Mad Scientists

On the table was a platter of steaming mashed potatoes. Melting pats of butter sent yellow rivulets down its craggy sides. Bright, orangey-red paprika was sprinkled on the peaks like a light snow on top of summer mountains.

The Bakers sat at the dinner table. Mr. Baker and Bracha stared gloomily at the creamy mound of potatoes. Mrs. Baker had her eyes closed; either she was thinking or asleep. Dina and Rivka were talking about that day's Chumash test, discussing which were the hardest questions and how they answered them. Zahava was deep in thought; she still didn't have a project for the Sewing Club. Yochie was trying to decide if she should shoot peas at the potato mountain with her fork. Tikva was reading a book. Since the book was in Braille, she could manage this under the table without anyone noticing.

Chezky, Donny, and Saraleh were playing "hands." First Saraleh would put down a hand, then Donny, then Chezky. Then Saraleh, Donny, and Chezky again. Then Saraleh would put her bottom hand on top, then Donny, then Chezky, faster and faster, until they were all slapping their hands on the table. Donny's water was in great danger of spilling.

Mrs. Baker opened her eyes. "Why aren't we eating?" she asked.

"Why, indeed," Mr. Baker responded, still staring at the potatoes.

"Why should we eat?" Bracha asked despondently.

"What do you mean, 'why should we eat'?" Mrs. Baker inquired.

"Where's Moishy?" Yochie said suddenly.

"Yes, where's Moishy?" Chezky echoed.

"He doesn't seem to be here," Mr. Baker observed. "Will someone go and get him?"

"I will," cried several voices, eager for an excuse to leave the table. Within one second, the dinner table was empty of children. They could be heard stampeding up the stairs, hollering "Moishy!" as they went.

"What happened?" Mrs. Baker asked.

"Zerizim makdimim lemitzvos?" Mr. Baker shrugged weakly.

"Jumping up to do mitzvos is all very well and good," said Mrs. Baker, "but this..." she waved her hand at the empty table. "You'd think they were running away from something."

Mr. Baker looked up at the ceiling. "Maybe I

should go, too," he said. Then, with a sigh, he reached for the big platter in the middle of the table. Holding it out to his wife he said, "Potatoes, dear?"

Upstairs, the Baker children found Moishy in the study, in front of the computer.

"Moi-shy, sup-per!" Dina informed him.

Moishy continued to stare at the screen.

"Moishy," said Dina. "Everyone is waiting for you."

Moishy continued to stare at the computer screen.

"Moishy," Rivka demanded. "What are you doing?"

Yochie pushed her way up to the computer screen. "Oh, he's playing that old game. You know, the one where you have to fit in the falling blocks."

"Moishy," Bracha asked him, "is this a time to be playing computer games?" She looked closer at the screen. "That's not our version. Where did you get this one, Moishy? Wait! It doesn't have blocks, it has letters. Hebrew letters, the Aleph-Beis! Neat! Where did you get this, Moishy?"

"Just a minute." He jotted something down on a pad and paused the game.

"Well?" Yochie asked impatiently.

"This, my friends," said Moishy with a flourish, "this is my Science Fair project."

"Moishy," Bracha said slowly, "did you program that game?"

"Yep!" Moishy said proudly.

"You didn't!" said Yochie.

"I don't believe it," said Rivka.

"Moishy, that's incredible!" Dina exclaimed.

"How do you play?" Chezky asked.

"I want to play! I want to play!" Saraleh jumped up and down.

Moishy patted her on the head. "It's not ready yet."

"It looks ready," Yochie insisted.

"I have to tighten up the programming a bit, and I need something from Ashi," Moishy told her.

"That's right, you and Ashi have spent all of his spare time with that box," said Rivka, pointing to the computer.

"SUPPER!"

"Oh! That's Abba," Saraleh exclaimed. The children ran downstairs.

"I think we should get those stairs reinforced," Mr. Baker commented to his wife as the children stampeded back into the room.

"Oh boy, potatoes again," Moishy cried with feigned enthusiasm.

"Very nice," Yochie agreed. They sat down and Mrs. Baker began to serve.

Zahava looked around the table with a critical eye while she waited for her food. "Moishy!" she said suddenly.

Moishy jumped. "What'd I do?" he asked.

"Whose sweater is that?" she demanded.

"What's this thing you have about sweaters?" Yochie asked.

"I wasn't talking to you," Zahava said rudely.

"Zahava," Mrs. Baker murmured.

"It's Ashi's," Moishy said. "He lets me wear it

because it has a hole in it."

"I noticed." Zahava looked at him, her fingers tapping impatiently on the table.

"Oh, for crying out loud, Zahava," Moishy said defensively. "I only wear it around the house."

"You shouldn't wear such a thing even around the house," Zahava told him.

"Will you stop trying to dress me?" Moishy said.

"Children!" Mr. Baker rumbled. Moishy made a face at Zahava. Zahava glowered but closed her mouth.

After everyone was eating, Mr. Baker turned to Moishy. "Well, young man," he asked, "what were you doing that kept you from this delicious supper?"

Yochie choked on a mouthful of potato. Dina banged her on the back.

"I was working on my project," Moishy answered. "The computer game I told you about."

Mr. Baker's eyes lit up. "And how's it going?"

"Oh, really good," said Moishy enthusiastically.

"What else do you have to do?" his father asked.

"Well," Moishy pursed his lips in thought. "There's a glitch or two in the program I just noticed; it shouldn't take more than a minute or two to fix up. Then all I have to do is wait for Ashi."

"Why do you have to wait for Ashi?" Rivka asked.

"He's got something for me," Moishy answered evenly. "A dictionary on a disk."

"Why do you need a dictionary?" Everyone was curious.

"You'll see," said Moishy mysteriously.

"You'll call me when you have a finished product?" Mr. Baker asked him. "I want to be the first to play. And you two," Mr. Baker continued, turning to Yochie and Chezky. "How is your project going?"

"Good! Great!" Yochie and Chezky answered, giggling.

"What's so funny?" Rivka demanded.

"Nothing much," Yochie and Chezky giggled some more.

"What are you people doing, anyway?" Rivka wanted to know. "You don't let anyone into the room where you're working, and you don't tell anyone anything. What are you making? What's it for?"

"It's very useful," Chezky informed her.

"A 'gold mine' of potential," said Yochie raising one finger. She managed to keep a straight face for a few seconds before breaking out into laughter once again.

The Baker family could get no more out of Chezky and Yochie, much to Rivka's frustration.

After dinner, Moishy ran to grab the computer before anyone else could. After ten minutes of intensive work at the keyboard, he was done. All he had to do now was wait for Ashi. Ashi knew someone who knew someone who had an uncle in computers, and he was going to supply the dictionary. The someone was supposed to bring it to the yeshiva this morning, and Ashi was supposed to make a special trip home tonight to give the disk to Moishy. Moishy made five backup copies of his precious program and went to his room to wait.

In his room, he flung himself down on his bed and picked up a book. After a few minutes, he put the book face down on the floor and lay back, staring up at the ceiling.

I can't wait, he thought. This is really going to be good. Moishy, my boy, you've done some worthy and wonderful projects in your time, but this is really the best. Yes, siree!

Rolling over on his side he looked over to Ashi's bed. Ashi had a lot to do with it, he admitted to himself. He's some brother, Ashi is. How many guys his age would even speak to their kid brothers, let alone help them out with some tricky programming! Getting that dictionary was really something, too! He smiled at Ashi's bed affectionately.

Stirring restlessly on the bed, Moishy looked around the room for something to do while he waited for Ashi. I really don't want to get involved with anything now; Ashi could be here any minute. Moishy got up and went to the door. Since he had nothing better to do, he wandered over to the homework room.

The homework room was empty except for Tikva practicing quietly at the piano. The old grand piano's deep tones resounded even when played softly.

Moishy stood quietly at the door, listening. With his good ear for music, he acutely appreciated his sister's playing; in such a short time she'd really gotten good. When he thought of her visual handicap he felt nothing short of awe.

She stopped playing. "Hi, Moishy," she said.

"How did you know I was here?" Moishy asked, surprised. "I was standing so quietly, right here by the door. No one can see the door from behind the piano. How did you know it was me?"

"Moishy," Tikva laughed. "Only you breathe so loud."

He clapped his hand over his nose — he hadn't realized that his breathing was as recognizable as his voice! He resolved to pay more attention to that in the future.

"What time is it?" he said.

Tikva lifted her wrist to let Moishy look at her watch. "It's 7:23," he said. She leaned her head to the side, listening to something. "There's someone at the front door. Could you..." she began, but Moishy was already out the door. What's his hurry? she wondered.

He ran down the steps two at a time and barreled into Rivka.

"Oof!" she blurted.

"Sorry, Rivka!" he shouted over his shoulder as he ran to the front door.

"It's about time you got here!" he shouted as he reached the door.

"Why, Moishy, I've never seen you so excited to see my friends!" Dina was standing at the door with her best friend, Idy Bodner.

"You're not Ashi!" was all he could say.

"I should say not!" Dina took her friend's arm and they went upstairs.

Moishy went out the door and stood in front of the

house. Where was Ashi? He looked up and down the street. Maybe he's not coming from the usual direction, maybe he had to stop somewhere first. A gray stationwagon turned the corner. Maybe he got a ride? Moishy looked at the stationwagon hopefully, but it cruised right past the house and down the street. He slumped against the doorpost. Ooourgh! he thought deep down inside. After a few more minutes, he turned and went back into the house. Picking up a book, he parked himself on the window seat, determined not to move until Ashi showed up.

One hour passed. No Ashi. Another half hour. Still no Ashi. Moishy closed his book and went into the kitchen for a drink.

Mrs. Baker was in the kitchen, making a cup of instant coffee and talking on the telephone.

"I don't know if I agree with you, Nava," she was saying. "I don't think a large format presentation is what we're interested in here...." Mrs. Baker absently put two spoons of sugar into her coffee. "Hang on a second," she said into the telephone. She made a *berachah* and took a sip of her coffee. "Ugh!" she grimaced. "I just put sugar in my coffee! I never take sugar; I must have thought I was making it for you!" She laughed.

Moishy realized that his mother was probably as familiar with the office staff's likes and dislikes as she was with those of her own family. He wasn't sure how he felt about that.

With a sigh, he went over to the refrigerator and helped himself to some juice. Taking his cup over to the kitchen table, he sat down and waited for his mother to finish on the telephone.

"Okay, Nava," she said. "I'll think about it. But you think about it, too. Try and picture what I'm talking about; tomorrow, I'll sketch it for you. Right! Good night." She hung up and turned to Moishy. "Hi, Moishy," she said. "Long time no see!"

"Yeah," Moishy agreed glumly.

"I've been so busy, I can hardly breathe," she commented. She looked at Moishy closely. "You look a bit down. What's the matter?"

Moishy made a face. "I'm fed up with waiting for Ashi."

"Waiting for Ashi?"

"Yeah," Moishy took another sip of his drink. "He was supposed to come tonight and bring me a disk that was really important for my project, and he hasn't come yet. I can't understand it." Moishy's face suddenly lit up. "I know, I'll call him." Mrs. Baker started to say something, but Moishy was already out of the room and dialing on the hall telephone.

He knew he had to let the telephone ring, and ring, and ring, but it was sheer torture. Finally, somebody answered.

"Hello?" said a voice.

"Hello," Moishy answered. "Is this the yeshiva?"

"This is a yeshiva," the voice replied. "Which one did you want?"

"This one. I'm looking for Ashi Baker."

"He's in my *shiur*."

"I'm his brother," Moishy informed the voice. "I need to speak to him. He's probably in the *beis midrash*."

"Aren't we all before a big test," said the voice. "I just came up here for a *sefer* I left in my room. I'll call him for you."

"What's your name?" asked Moishy, curious about who he was speaking to. But it was too late, the owner of the voice was gone.

After what seemed like a lifetime, someone picked up the telephone. "Hello?"

"Ashi!"

"Moishy, hi! What's up?"

"That's what I want to ask you," said Moishy, exasperated. "Why didn't you show up with the disk?"

"I called last night to say I wasn't coming," Ashi informed him.

"What?" Moishy couldn't believe his ears.

"I have a big test," Ashi explained. "There's no way I can leave the yeshiva right now. I don't know when I can come."

"Oh." Moishy was crushed.

"But I called and left you a message," said Ashi. "Didn't Ima give you the message?"

"Something must have happened; I didn't get the message."

"Sorry, kid," said Ashi sympathetically. "I gotta run. I'll get that disk to you soon, don't you worry."

"Okay, Ashi," said Moishy. "*Behatzlachah* on your test."

"Thanks, Moishy. Bye!"

"Bye!" Moishy hung up the telephone and dragged himself back to the kitchen. His mother was still there.

"What is it, Moishy? What's wrong?"

"You didn't give me the message. Ashi's not coming."

Mrs. Baker looked at her son. "Moishy, I'm sorry. Ashi asked me to tell you that he couldn't make it and I forgot. I'm so sorry."

Moishy stared at his mother. He could see the distress in her eyes. He forced himself to speak in a light tone. "It's okay Ima. Don't worry about it."

"Maybe I can arrange for Abba to pick it up," she suggested.

Moishy got up. "No, don't worry about it," he said. "It's getting late and I'm tired. I think I'll go to bed. G'night, Ima." He kissed her lightly on the cheek and went upstairs.

As he walked into his room, he closed the door carefully behind him. He stood behind the door and stared across the room at Ashi's bed. So he's not coming, he thought. And Ima knew the whole time. I waited the whole night and Ima knew the whole time; she forgot to tell me. I went crazy waiting. Ima knew and she just forgot. She didn't forget to call her boss, but she forgot me.

After supper, Yochie and Chezky had zoomed upstairs and secreted themselves in Chezky's room with an "Authorized Personnel Only" sign on the door. There was another sign that said "Stay Out" and a third that said "This Means You." When Rivka tried to follow them into the room, she was shown the signs. The door was closed firmly in her face.

"A chutzpah!" she fumed as she stalked down to the kitchen to do the dinner dishes.

Usually, Rivka didn't mind doing the dishes. Often, she even enjoyed it. But tonight, as she scrubbed and slipped the dishes in and out of the hot, soapy water, she was really not in the mood.

As Rivka was finishing the forks and knives, Yochie slid through the door. "I beg your pardon," she said as she skipped across the room.

"What do you want?" Rivka asked.

"Oh, just a broom," Yochie replied and skipped out of the room again.

As she was rinsing the pots, Chezky crept in. "Don't mind me," he said.

"I'll try not to,' Rivka muttered.

"You haven't seen that old radio of Abba's have you? The one he used to listen to over breakfast?" Chezky asked her.

"No, I haven't," Rivka told him. "What do you need it for?"

"Something," Chezky informed her. "I'll go and look in the study." He left, letting the kitchen door swing shut behind him.

"What is going on?" Rivka wondered. She marched up the stairs and into her room. There, lying on the beds and reading, were Dina, Tikva, and Zahava.

"Do you know what Yochie and Chezky are doing for the Science Fair project?" she demanded of them.

"Nope," said Tikva.

"Double nope," said Dina.

"Triple nope," said Zahava. She yawned and turned the page.

Rivka stamped her foot. "They're running around the house giggling like maniacs and locking themselves up! They collect all sorts of weird things and they disappear! Don't you people care?"

"I couldn't care less!" Zahava exclaimed

Tikva looked up at Rivka. "I care, but I doubt that I could get them to tell us." Dina nodded in agreement. "We'll know sooner or later," she added.

"I don't think they have a right to keep it from us," Rivka said. "We're family."

"Good luck," Zahava commented.

"Don't you want to do anything about this?" Rivka was livid.

"Nope," said Tikva.

"Double nope," said Dina.

"Triple n..." But before Zahava could add her voice to the chorus, Rivka was out the door.

In the hall, she bumped into Moishy.

"Ouch!" she said. "Sorry."

"No problem, Rivka," he shouted over his shoulder as he skirted her and ran off.

Rivka rubbed her arm as she watched his retreating back. There was no use trying to get him involved, she thought, he was too busy with his own project.

Determined to get to the bottom of this, Rivka went down the hall and put her ear to Chezky's door.

"Chezky, don't..." she heard Yochie's muffled voice say. "Chezky, I can't believe you did that!" She heard a metallic clank and giggles.

"What is going on in there?" She put her ear against the keyhole. She heard voices, laughter, and a few shrieks. "What could be so funny about a science project?" she said out loud. Suddenly, the door flew open and Rivka almost fell in the room.

"Rivka!" Yochie exclaimed. "What are you doing here?" Without waiting for a reply, Yochie continued, "Well, since you're here, how about a bobby pin?" Embarrassed and confused, Rivka took a bobby pin from her hair and handed it to her sister.

"Thanks!" Yochie turned and went into the room, closing the door firmly behind her.

Rivka stood and stared at the door, but without X-ray vision, there was no way she could find out what they were doing in there. Rivka, like the rest of the Bakers, would just have to wait.

9
Council of War

Cold rain beat against the slightly foggy window pane in the quintuplets' room. Outside it was gray, the kind of gray weather that turns the whole world gray with it. Moishy stared at the window humming to himself, "...Whether the weather be cold or whether the weather be hot, we'll weather the weather, whatever the weather, whether we like it or not."

"Moishy, what are you muttering?"

"Nothing. It doesn't look like he's coming tonight either," Moishy complained.

"Who?" Zahava asked.

"Ashi," he replied. "With my disk."

"Oh."

In a moment of desperation, Zahava had asked Moishy for a little help with her math homework. Moishy, the genius, knew math far above his grade level when he wanted to. Now she couldn't get rid of him. He was sitting in her room and complaining and driving her crazy.

"I can't believe he didn't show up," he went on. "And I can't believe that Ima didn't tell me."

Zahava was sprawled on her bed with her books. Moishy was next to her bed on the floor. Zahava twisted around until she could look Moishy in the eye. "Moishy, trust me, you'll get the disk," she said. She turned back to her books.

"That's not the point," Moishy said. "The point is..."

Zahava slammed her book shut. "Finished! " she said with relish.

"Mazal tov," said Moishy glumly. He put his head in his hands and stared across the room.

Rivka walked in, followed by Dina and Tikva. "...And they still won't tell anyone," she was saying.

"We knew they wouldn't," Tikva told her. "We'll find out what they're doing sooner or later. Hi, Zahava. Hi, Moishy," she said to the room's occupants.

"Hi," said Zahava.

"Low," said Moishy.

"Can you stop being such a grouch?" Zahava demanded.

"No," Moishy replied with a sigh.

Tikva walked over to her bed and picked up a book lying there. She put her pillow against the wall, leaned on it, and with a happy sigh, began to read. Dina sat down and started writing in her diary. Rivka paced back and forth across the floor.

"If only we had a hint, I'm sure we could figure out what's going on." She thought for a moment, then stopped in front of Moishy. "Moishy, I appoint you my spy."

"I'm currently unavailable," he informed her.

"What do you mean?" Rivka didn't believe him.

"I'm not available for spying," Moishy said. "Besides, if I had a secret project, I wouldn't want anyone spying on me."

Rivka opened her mouth and closed it again. If it was Yochie planning this, you can bet that he would go along, she thought. What's she got that I don't have? She walked to the door and was about to walk out when she heard Chezky and Yochie coming toward the room, talking. Rivka decided to stay put and try to hear what they were saying.

"Once we get the tray attached, then we're practically done," Yochie said.

"But what about that switch, you know, the one that keeps coming loose?" Chezky asked her.

"We'll take care of it, don't worry." She stopped suddenly. "Shh!" she said. "Someone might hear."

Humph! Rivka thought as she moved back from the door. Yochie and Chezky strolled cheerily into the room.

"Hello, everybody!" they said.

Zahava looked up. "Oh, it's the mad scientists." She put her head in her hands again.

"How's it going?" Tikva asked them.

Yochie cackled and rubbed her hands while Chezky,

playing the part of the mad scientist's assistant, hunched up one shoulder and limped across the room. "It's going fine," he lisped. "Aha, aha, aha!" he laughed gruesomely.

"Oh, Chezky, stop that!" Rivka snapped.

"Sorry, Maaaster," he leered.

"Chezky, really!" Zahava said irritably.

"Really what?" Bracha asked, walking into the room. She looked around. "What's this, a conference?"

"Yes," Yochie cackled. "It's the Semi-Annual Meeting of Mad Scientists and Great Inventors. I'm the Chairman." She gestured at Chezky. "Igor, here, is the Master of Ceremonies."

Chezky limped over to Bracha and offered his hand. "How do you doooo?" he intoned.

Bracha hunched up one shoulder and crossed her eyes. "Fine, thanks, and you?" she said in a gravelly voice. Most of the children laughed appreciatively. Zahava glowered.

Bracha turned to Dina. "Actually I didn't really come here for a conference. Are you done with the new book yet?"

"Yep," Dina replied. "I'll get it for you." She went to the dresser to get the book. "That's funny, it's not here."

"Can you smell ammonia?" Yochie asked her. "Maybe the book dissolved."

"Yochie!"

"Seriously, it's getting impossible to find anything around here," Yochie said.

"I hate to admit it, but it's true," Dina said. "I even heard Abba complaining. Zahava went and cleaned out his office."

"Who?" Zahava asked.

"Zahava/Zlata," Dina explained.

"Zlata, Zlata, Zlata! Her name is Zlata!" Zahava pounded her pillow for emphasis.

"Touchy, touchy!" Yochie made a tsk-tsk noise with her tongue.

"Touchy?" Zahava returned. "At least I don't go around touching other people's things!"

"Yeah, what's wrong with you these days?" Bracha asked. "Did you figure out a project for your Sewing Club yet?"

"No, not yet." Zahava slumped on her bed.

"What's so hard about a sewing project?" Moishy wanted to know.

"Shows how much you know," Zahava told him.

"Ask a simple question..." Moishy muttered. "I was asking because I was interested." Moishy crossed his arms over his chest.

"Since when are you interested in sewing?" Zahava snapped back.

"You know, you spend the whole week talking about everyone's clothing and redressing them, and then I bring it up and you get mad!" Moishy glared at her.

"Moishy! Zahava!" Bracha warned them. Deciding that it was a good time to change the subject, she turned to Yochie and Chezky. "How's your thing going?" she asked.

"Good!" "Great!" they said simultaneously.

"Whatever it is," said Rivka, rolling her eyes to the ceiling.

"Oh, it's a 'neat' project all right," said Chezky.

"When you see it, you'll be 'automatically' excited," Yochie giggled.

"It will push all the right buttons!" Chezky guffawed.

"We should win the first prize at the Fair in one clean sweep!" Yochie shrieked, and she and Chezky dissolved into loud laughter.

The other children looked at each other, puzzled.

"What is so funny?!" Rivka roared. Yochie and Chezky only laughed harder.

"I hope I get my project done on time," Moishy moaned when they had calmed down.

"Oh, Moishy," Dina reassured him. "You've got tons of time. Ashi will get that disk to you."

"If only Ima told me that Ashi wasn't coming, maybe I could have thought of another plan."

"Will you stop moaning about that already," said Zahava, sitting up in bed.

"You should talk," Moishy returned.

"What do you mean, I should talk?" Zahava asked.

"You spend the whole day moaning about your long-lost closet and your Sewing Club," Moishy told her, standing up and brushing off imaginary dust. "At least I'm involved in something important!"

Zahava turned bright red. "Something important!" she fumed. "Something important! The boy genius, here, thinks the only important thing in this world are bytes and chips!"

"Potato?" Yochie asked irreverently.

"He can sit all day staring at a monitor, and he can't even tuck in his shirt!" Zahava stood up and looked pointedly at his untucked shirttail and droopy corduroys.

"I've had it with you and your clothes!" Moishy raged, and in one quick movement, he shoved Zahava. She lost her balance and sat down hard on the floor.

There was a stunned silence. The air was charged with tension. Everyone stared at Moishy and Zahava; no one could believe what had just happened. A Baker never hit or pushed another Baker, or anyone. Even the smallest members of the family knew that.

Zahava stayed on the floor as if she were frozen to the spot, her face pale. Moishy's was red and he was breathing hard. His fists were clenched. He looked around the room defensively. "She started it," he said.

"Moishy!" Bracha said in a hushed, shocked voice.

"Zahava, are you okay?" Dina went over to her sister and gave her a hand up.

"I'm okay," she muttered, giving Moishy a guarded look. There was an awkward silence; no one knew what to say.

Slowly, Moishy's breathing slowed and his color returned to normal. He stood looking at his feet.

"Moishy?" Bracha said softly. Moishy waved his hand at her as if to shoo her away. He went over to Zahava.

"Look, Zahava," he said. "Look, I'm sorry. I shouldn't have shoved you. I'm sorry."

Zahava's face softened. She cleared her throat. "You know, we're taught that when we want to criticize someone for something, we should really look at ourselves. I guess I was being pretty annoying. I'm sorry, too." She smiled a tentative smile at him.

He returned a broad grin. He felt like he ought to hug her or something. Instead, he suddenly stuck out his hand. "Friends?"

Zahava laughed, took his hand, and shook it. "Friends," she agreed. The last of the tense atmosphere in the room dissolved.

"That was well done," Bracha told them. "Ima and Abba would be proud of you."

"None of this would have happened if Ima was here," Yochie declared.

"What do you mean?" Bracha asked her.

"I mean that everything went from great to bad to worse since Ima went to work," Yochie explained. "The mood in the house has been awful. This fight is just a symptom of the general disease."

"Disease?" Dina asked.

"No-Ima-itis," Yochie informed her.

"Thank you, Dr. Yochie," Tikva laughed.

"I think Yochie's right," Zahava said. Everyone nodded his head in agreement. Encouraged, she went on, "And I think we should do something about it!"

"Let's talk about it to Abba," Dina suggested. "It's always good to talk."

"But I did talk to Abba about it," said Zahava.

"When?" Rivka interrupted.

"The other night," Zahava told her. "After my clothes were...um, after something happened." She looked at Moishy, who grinned back.

"And?"

"Basically, he just told me to be patient." She sighed.

"Well, then it's time we did something ourselves!" Yochie declared.

"Yeah!" Zahava agreed.

"Let's hold a meeting!" Rivka said excitedly. She ran to get a pad and pen. "Sit down everyone," she commanded.

"Who put you in charge?" Yochie asked her.

"You did," Rivka said.

"I did?" Yochie squeaked. "When? How?"

"By letting me be born first." Rivka wrote down on her pad: Baker Conference, Children's Division.

"Where did I hear that before?" Yochie wondered.

"Actually, I was born first," said Bracha.

"Oh," said Rivka. She sat for a moment with the pad on her lap. Then, slowly, she held it out to Bracha. "I guess you should have this."

Everyone stared at Rivka in disbelief; she'd never given in like that before! Bracha found that once Rivka gave in, it was easier to give herself. "Actually, you're better at these things than me, Rivka," she said. Rivka smiled and kept the pad.

"We should have recorded this," Yochie whispered.

"Shhhh!" Tikva hushed her.

"Ahem!" Rivka cleared her throat. "This meeting is now called to order!"

"Hear! Hear!" Yochie crowed.

"Shhhh!"

"We will now have Moishy Baker state clearly what the purpose of this meeting is." Rivka pointed at Moishy with her pencil.

Moishy stood up and put his hands behind his back. "A few weeks ago, our mother entered the ranks of the employed, leaving her offspring to fend for themselves in a state of too much responsibility. While said pressures were somewhat ameliorated by the employment of a caretaker, whose country of origin is the former Union of Soviet Socialist Republics, nevertheless, said employment necessitated the consumption of altogether too much *Solanum tuberosum* in all its varied forms, and the odorousness of NH4 pervading our domicile, not to mention the havoc caused by said caretaker's ministrations in the area of the domestic arts. Therefore, we have decided to gather together in order to seek solutions to this difficult and dire situation." Moishy gave a little bow and sat down.

"What?" Yochie exclaimed.

"Yeah, what?" Chezky echoed.

Rivka pointed her pencil at Tikva. "Tikva, will you translate, please?"

"Ima went to work, and there was too much to do. Zlata was hired, and now we eat too many potatoes, everything smells like ammonia, and we can't find a everything smells like ammonia, and we can't find a thing. We're looking for ideas on how to solve this problem."

"Thank you, Tikki..."

"Really!" Yochie interrupted.

"And now," said Rivka, her pencil hovering over her pad, "are there any suggestions?"

"Let's kidnap Ima!" Yochie shouted.

"Let's blow up Sefer Press!" Chezky suggested.

"I think we should strike," Zahava put in.

"Yeah," said Moishy. "We could make signs and picket, and shout, 'We Want Ima!' "

"Don't be ridiculous, we can't go on strike," Bracha scolded. "I think that we should call Safta, and she could tell Ima to stop working."

"I think we should try to talk to Ima and Abba once again," said Dina.

"...Go on strike," Rivka was busy writing. "Call Safta. Speak to parents." She looked up. "Any more suggestions?"

"Buried treasure," said Chezky. "We should find buried treasure."

"How would that help?" Rivka asked him.

"Then we'd have enough money, and Ima wouldn't have to work," Chezky explained.

Rivka looked at him a moment. Then she wrote, "Buried treasure."

"Anything else?" There was a moment's silence. "I guess not. Okay, let's go over this list."

"I think we can skip that first item," said Zahava.

"Kidnapping Ima?"

"Yes, even if we succeeded in kidnapping her, we really couldn't keep her a prisoner," Zahava explained.

"It was a joke," Yochie said.

"Can we assume that items number two and three were jokes, too?" Rivka asked.

"Blowing up Sefer Press is a good idea, it's just not so practical," Chezky said.

"No kidding!" Dina rolled her eyes toward the ceiling. "I really think..."

"What's wrong with a strike?" Moishy wanted to know.

"Moishy," said Tikva patiently. "What do you think Ima and Abba would think of such an idea?"

Moishy thought for a minute. "Not much, I guess. But maybe that would be the reason it would work. When they see how badly we behave..."

"Really, Moishy!" Bracha exclaimed. "What about telling Safta?"

"Maybe that would work," said Rivka thoughtfully.

"I don't think it's a good idea to pull someone else into this," Tikva said. "Besides, Safta doesn't tell Ima what to do; she's not a little girl anymore. And Safta would worry."

"Scratch that idea," said Rivka, crossing it off on her pad. "We don't want to worry Safta."

"Now that we've gotten rid of all those crazy ideas..." Dina began.

"I'd even be happy if we could just get rid of Zlata,"

Moshe said quickly.

"Now that would be a start," Rivka said. "It wouldn't be a whole solution but..."

"I, for one, don't want to go back to crazy mornings and too-busy afternoons!" Bracha interrupted. "What would we do without Zlata?"

Chezky and Yochie had been eyeing each other during the conversation. Finally, Chezky nodded at Yochie, and Yochie smiled. "We think we have a solution to that," she said.

"What are you talking about?" Rivka demanded.

"Wait here a minute," said Yochie. "We'll be right back." She and Chezky ran out of the room.

"What are they up to now?" Rivka asked.

Tikva shrugged. "Who knows?"

They heard a commotion down the hall, followed by giggles and the sound of jumping feet.

"Whatever it is, Donny and Saraleh like it." Zahava went to the door and looked out into the hall. Her jaw dropped. "I don't believe it," she said. "I just don't believe it!" She clapped her hand over her mouth and danced back into the room.

Rivka jumped up and was about to go and look too, when, at the door, appeared the strangest thing she'd ever seen. It was about her height and boxlike in shape. In an arm projecting from one side, it had a broom, in another, a dustpan. In front was a tray with a small vase of flowers standing on it. Over its front were knobs and blinking lights, and it wore an old hat. Rolling smoothly, it came over the carpet toward her.

"Wow!" Moishy exclaimed. "A robot!"

"Stop it!" Rivka shrieked, jumping on a bed. "It's coming right at me!"

Yochie appeared at the door, followed by Chezky, Donny, and Saraleh. The little Bakers were thrilled by this gigantic new toy.

"Help!" Rivka yelled. "Stop it!" The rest of the Bakers rolled with laughter. Yochie pushed a button on a remote control panel in her hand and the robot stopped, right in front of Rivka. "You wanted to know what we were doing, Rivka, " she said with a mischievous smile. "Well, meet Zahava 3."

"What?!" shrieked Zahava.

"Well," Yochie explained. "Zlata is Zahava 2, right?"

"No!" Zahava exclaimed.

"So this is Zahava 3!" Yochie smiled toothily at her sister.

"Yochie, if you dare..." Zahava threatened.

"I have an idea," Moishy interrupted. "Let's call her Goldie."

"Goldie?"

"Why not? It's Yiddish for Zahava and Zlata," he explained.

"Great!" Chezky exclaimed. Zahava groaned and hid her face.

"Seriously, Yochie," Bracha said. "Where did you get this?"

"Well, you know Abba gets all kinds of magazines that have to do with his work as a patent attorney," Yochie told them. "One day I was in his study with him, and he said to me, 'Hey, Yochie look at this,' so I looked and there was an ad for a do-it-yourself robot kit. Well, I thought it was really neat, and I could see that Abba thought so too, so I asked him to order it and he did. The ad said that it would take a couple of months to come, and I forgot all about it until this Science Fair came up. The package came just in time!" She turned to Rivka. "Now you know what we've been doing all this time."

"Now I know!" Rivka repeated with a wry grin.

"But I don't see how this is going to help us with our 'Zlata' problem," Zahava complained.

"Look," said Chezky eagerly. "It can do all kinds of things to help around the house. It can sweep," he said, pointing to the broom and dustpan. "It can carry things on its tray," he said, pointing to the small vase with flowers. "It didn't spill a drop! And look at this!" He pushed a button, got down on his hands and knees, and pointed at the carpet. Right next to the floor, from a hole in the side of the robot, came a spray of water. After the spray finished, the robot rolled forward, made a sort of grinding noise, and rolled back again. "The spray is a cleaning solution, and under the robot are little rubber scrubbing wheels. It can clean, too!"

There were exclamations of wonder and surprise.

"Neat!" Moishy exclaimed.

"We may not be able to bring Ima back, but with Zahava 3, I mean Goldie, we can get rid of Zlata and still keep the house clean!" Yochie grinned expectantly.

"That's right," Zahava agreed, seeing the potential in the situation.

"And you won't put ammonia in her shpritzer!" said Moishy.

"I should say not, " Yochie looked offended.

"But..." Dina tried to get their attention.

"How does the broom work?" Donny asked.

Yochie demonstrated the broom. "Again!" Saraleh cried.

Carried away, Yochie grabbed a container of talcum powder and dumped half of it on the rug.

"Yochie!"

"Just you watch!" she cried. She pressed a button on the remote control. Goldie started to sweep up the powder, sending clouds of it up in the air on either side of her. She then scrubbed the spot where the powder had been.

"One of these days, Yochie..." Rivka said, coughing from all the powder in the air.

"Can I say something?" Dina asked.

"Why, yes, Dina," said Tikva. "You've been trying to say something all this time."

"Thank you," said Dina, obviously relieved. "Listen, this robot is really great, and while I don't quite see how it can do all of the housework, like cooking..."

"We haven't worked out all of the kinks yet," Yochie said defensively.

"Anyway," Dina continued, determined not to be cut off. "It still doesn't solve the Ima problem."

The children looked at the robot and realized that

Dina was right.

"There's always buried treasure," Chezky sighed.

"I still think that we should try to speak to Abba and Ima, or at least Ima," Dina urged them. "They've always listened to us before, so let's try once more."

The children thought for a moment.

"You're right, Dini," said Tikva. Dina looked at her sister gratefully.

"I agree," said Bracha.

"When I went to Abba, I really went for myself, not for all of us," Zahava mentioned.

"We should try once more," said Rivka clapping her fist into her other hand. The rest of the children nodded in agreement. Rivka announced: "The Baker Conference, Children's Division, has unanimously decided to confer with their parents about the problem." She looked everyone. "Tomorrow?" she asked.

"Tomorrow!" they agreed.

"I hereby declare this meeting adjourned!"

10
Enough Is Enough!

It was only after the meeting was over that the Baker children realized they would have to appoint someone to talk with Ima. After some deliberation, it was decided that Bracha would represent all of the children.

"After all, she is the oldest," said Dina.

"While Ashi is in yeshiva," Rivka put in. Giving in to Bracha's leadership still wasn't easy.

Bracha woke up early and padded over to the window. It was a very early spring day the kind the weatherman called "partly cloudy." Rotund cumulis clouds sailed across a pale blue sky, their round shadows moving smoothly over the ground below them. The leaves and branches of the trees swayed and bowed in the breeze; it looked like the shadows of the clouds were pushing them, not the wind.

Bracha leaned on the windowsill and looked out,

deep in thought. How could she get Ima to listen, she wondered. Rehearsing little speeches in her head, she imagined herself speaking to her mother: "Ima, we love you and are proud of the job you are doing, but things aren't really working out...." Or maybe: "Ima, all of the kids asked me to speak to you in their name...." Maybe we need something a bit more up front: "Let's face it, Ima, things haven't been the same around here...." No, that sounded too mean.

Bracha sighed and reached for her robe. As she was pulling it on, she heard her mother in the hall. With one arm halfway up a sleeve, she ran out to meet her.

"Ima," she whispered.

Mrs. Baker turned around. "Good morning, Bracha. You're up bright and early!"

Bracha smiled. "I guess so," she said.

"I can't believe it's Thursday already, there's so much to do," her mother smiled.

"Yes, there is," Bracha agreed. "Ima, if you have a minute, I'd like to speak to you."

From down the hall, Rachel Ahuva wailed. "In a couple of minutes, honey. The baby's crying," Mrs. Baker told her. "I like it when she wakes up early, I get to spend a little time with her." Mrs. Baker went down the hall to the baby's room. "Why don't you get dressed first and we'll talk over breakfast," she said over her shoulder.

"Okay," Bracha went back to her room and got dressed.

As she was brushing her hair, Rivka poked her head in the door. "Did you talk?" she asked.

"Not yet," said Bracha.

"What are you waiting for?"

"This is easier said than done!" Bracha slammed the brush down on the dresser and pushed past Rivka out of the room.

Down in the kitchen, her mother was feeding the baby. "Help yourself to breakfast and come and sit down," she said. "I have time to talk now."

Bracha grabbed cereal and milk and sat down. "Ima listen...."

"Mmmm?" Mrs. Baker took a sip of her coffee.

"All of us were talking and..." Donny chased Saraleh into the kitchen shrieking with laughter. Saraleh tripped and he fell right on top of her, turning the laughter into tears. Mrs. Baker jumped up and ran to the small children.

"There, there," she said as she kissed them better. "Don't play so wild, okay?" Donny and Saraleh tearfully agreed and sat down to eat breakfast.

"Right, Bracha," said Mrs. Baker sitting down again. "What were you saying?"

"All of us..." Bracha began again. The telephone rang.

"I'm sorry, *zeeskeit*, but this might be important. Why would anyone call at this hour?" Mrs. Baker said as she jumped up to answer it. While she was talking, Zahava walked into the room.

"Did you talk to her yet?" she asked Bracha.

"I'm trying!" Bracha rolled her eyes toward the telephone. Zahava nodded understandingly.

Mrs. Baker hung up the telephone. "That was Zlata," she said. "She's going to be a little late today, but I think we'll manage. Bracha..."

"I'll make the sandwiches." Zahava jumped up. "You and Bracha sit, it looked like you were in the middle of talking or something."

"Thank you, Zahava," Mrs. Baker said, delighted by this unexpected assistance. "It really isn't easy to have a talk around here." She looked at her watch. "It looks like we have about five minutes. Will that be enough?"

"Yes," Bracha said quickly as she swallowed the last of her breakfast. "We waited a long time before..."

Mr. Baker walked in the door, back from minyan. "Shoshana, I'm glad I caught you," he said. "Sorry, Bracha, but I need Ima. I wanted to discuss the last bill for the work on the house." Bracha waited as her parents began to talk finances.

As she was sitting and waiting, Moishy walked in, followed by the rest of the family. "Nu?" he said.

"Nu!" she answered, indicating her parents deep in conversation.

"Nu," Moishy sighed, and helped himself to breakfast.

While their parents talked, the children finished eating and getting ready for school, making sure that everything was ready early so there would be time to talk. Finally, Mr. Baker said, "Right, so we have that clear. I guess that's that." He looked around the room. "What's everyone standing around for?" he asked.

Mrs. Baker caught sight of the kitchen clock. "Oh no, I'm late! Bye everyone!" She grabbed her handbag and ran out the door. Everyone looked after her with long faces.

"Well," Mr. Baker said, "I thought that with Zlata late we'd have a bit of a runaround, but I see that everything is all set. I'm proud of you kids." He pinched Saraleh's cheek, ruffled Chezky's hair, and, humming to himself, he went out of the kitchen.

The children stood around avoiding eye contact and feeling let down. After a short time, Tikva said, "Well, Bracha, you tried."

"I think I'll try to climb Mount Everest tomorrow!" She picked up her school bag. "Come on, we might as well go to school." The Baker children filed slowly out of the house and up the street.

At least school went well for Bracha that day. There was an assembly and the principal spoke. She loved to hear Rebbitzin Falovitz speak. Then she got back a math test with a good grade, and a Chumash test with 100% blazoned across the top. Lunchtime was really funny when her friend Estie told them how, last summer, her Uncle Shmuel found a skunk in his car. On the way home, she arranged with her best friend Yehudis, to go out for pizza the coming week.

Bracha was feeling much more optimistic by the time she got home. After all, she thought as she ran up the steps, the morning is really a crazy time to try to talk to anyone.

The kitchen was empty. Bracha grabbed a few cookies and ran up to the homework room. I'll finish my homework now before Ima comes home, she thought.

Her homework took her longer than she expected. When she finished, she looked up at the clock and was surprised at how much time had passed. She packed up her books and ran down to the kitchen.

Zlata was there, along with Tikva, Dina, and Saraleh. "Hello," said Zlata cheerfully.

"Hello," Bracha answered uncertainly. She wanted to ask where Ima was, but she worried that if she asked right away, she might hurt Zlata's feelings.

"Ima called," Tikva told her. "She's going to be late."

"Again!" Saraleh sighed such a big, grown-up sigh that Bracha had to laugh. As she gave Saraleh a little hug, she thought how nice it was to have a sister like Tikva who practically read her mind.

The telephone rang. Bracha was halfway up out of her chair when Moishy burst through the kitchen door from the outside. "I'll get it!" he shouted. "Hello! Baker residence, Moishy Baker speaking. May I help you?" He stood for a minute, breathing hard. "Hello, Abba!" he said into the telephone. "Fine, *baruch Hashem*, how are you?...Uh, huh...I just got home. One sec, I'll check." He put his hand over the receiver. "Is Ima home?"

"Nope," Dina informed him. "She'll be working

late. She's not sure when she'll get in."

"No such luck, Abba," Moishy spoke into the telephone. "Okay...bye!" He held out the receiver. "Zahava, my father wants to speak to you." Zlata took the telephone. While she spoke to Mr. Baker, Moishy complained.

"Abandoned again!" he moaned. "No father, no mother! We're practically orphans!"

"*Chas veshalom!*" Dina gasped. "Really, Moishy!"

"So much for speaking to either of our parents today," Bracha said glumly.

"I'm sure you'll have a chance when they get home," Tikva reassured her.

"I hope so," Bracha said. She sauntered over to the back door and glumly looked out. It was still gray outside and just starting to rain. Perfect weather, wet and depressing, she thought.

Zlata hung up the telephone. She told the children, "Since the Abba and the Ima are late, I will stay a little late too."

"You don't have to," Bracha told her.

"Your Abba say I stay," she said.

"Well, thank you Zlata, um, Zahava," said Bracha.

Zlata saw the children's faces. "Don't be sad, " she said. "I will make special food — a special dish from England. You will like it very much."

The children brightened when they heard this. Maybe Zlata was finally going to make something without potatoes!

"Okay, Zla...uh, Zahava," said Moishy.

Bracha stood up. "Well," she said. "Since I've finished my homework, I might as well practice the piano."

"Might as well," Tikva agreed. "I'll go after you." Zlata beamed at them. Bracha left the kitchen.

The late afternoon was mostly quiet, the rain pattering against the windows as the family went about their business. The only exciting moment was when Yochie sent Goldie into the kitchen to bring back dishes that she'd used to eat a snack in her room. Zlata screamed and then burst out laughing. The whole family came running to see what the commotion was about.

"When I first see," Zlata told them, wiping tears of laughter from her eyes, "I think it is from...how do you say...?" She pointed to the ceiling.

"Upstairs?" Dina asked her.

"Outer space?" Moishy suggested. "Mars?"

Zlata pointed at him. "Yes," she said. "From Mars."

"I'll leave her here to help you," Yochie said generously.

"She no take me up there?" Zlata joked. "To...space?"

"I won't let her, Zlata, don't you worry," Yochie reassured her.

Moishy pranced over to the oven. "When will the English dish be ready?" he asked, sniffing appreciatively.

"For supper," Zlata said firmly. She pointed to the door. "Now go. I have much to do." She turned to the robot. "You can leave her," she said, putting a bottle of ammonia on Goldie's tray. "She will help." The children giggled and filed out of the kitchen.

"Poor Goldie," Yochie whispered to Chezky. "I hope ammonia doesn't corrode her circuits."

Dinner time found all of the Bakers crowded around the table eagerly waiting for the new dish.

"I wonder what it is?" Chezky whispered.

"I once heard that the English like lamb in mint sauce," Moishy said.

"Mint sauce!" Chezky said. "Ugh!"

"I'll eat anything other than potatoes!" Moishy said emphatically.

"Even mint sauce?"

"Well, I'd try it, anyway," Moishy sniffed the air. "But this doesn't smell like mint sauce." His stomach growled.

"Mmmmmm!" Chezky agreed, sighting Zlata coming towards them with a large, covered casserole dish.

"Here is new dish," she announced. She lifted off the cover. "Shepherd's Pie!" The children leaned forward to see.

"Shepherd's Pie!" Bracha exclaimed without thinking. "That's made with mashed potatoes!" There was a stunned silence.

Zlata, unaware of the children's distress, took up the plates and began to serve up generous portions of Shepherd's Pie. When she put Moishy's plate in front of him, he stared at the pile of potatoes and meat. Then something snapped. "I can't eat this," he said.

"Me neither," Yochie groaned. "If I look at one

more potato, I think I'm going to die."

"Shhh!" Bracha hissed at her.

"We've had it with potatoes!" Rivka exclaimed. "Had it!"

"Rivka!" Dina exclaimed in shock.

"I hate potatoes," said Donny, fiercely kicking the table leg.

"I hope I never see another potato! Never!" Zahava declared sitting back and crossing her arms.

Bracha jumped up and took the serving spoon out of Zlata's hand. "I'll serve," she said. "Why don't you go and get some soda from the pantry." Startled and confused, Zlata went to the pantry.

"Have you guys gone out of your minds?" she demanded of her brothers and sisters in a fierce whisper.

"Yes," Moishy shot back. "Potato crazy! This is the limit."

"Yeah!" said Donny.

"It's crazy to eat potatoes all day, every day!" Zahava exclaimed.

"Yeah!" said Donny.

"Potatoes make me throw up!" Chezky stood up and clutched at his stomach.

"Yeah!" said Donny.

"No potatoes!" Saraleh shouted.

"Yeah!" said Donny, banging his fist on the table.

"I know what I'm going to do," Yochie said, jumping up from her chair. She raced over to the bread box and took out the bread. She then climbed up to the cupboard and took out the peanut butter and went to the refrigerator and took out the jelly. Sighting Goldie standing quietly on the side of the kitchen, she put the bread in one of her "hands" and the peanut butter and jelly on her tray. "See!" she said. "We don't need Zlata." She pushed a button on the remote control and Goldie began to roll toward the table.

"That's right!" Chezky yelled. "We don't need her." He ran over to the fogged-up window and wrote in bold letters "ZLATA GO HOME!" Moishy cheered. Dina ran toward the window to erase the sign, but it was too late.

Zlata came from the pantry just in time to see Chezky scrawl his message on the window. She stood stock still, staring at the sign, shocked and hurt. She placed the bottles of soda on the table as tears came to her eyes.

"I see," she said in a choked voice. "I see what goes on. You kids...you kids...you don't understand.... You know, I was scientist in Russia, yes, a good one, computer scientist, better than this," she said, gesturing to the robot. She took out a handkerchief, wiped her eyes, and blew her nose. "I am happy, no problems. Then one day, I come home. There is a big sign, in paint, on my door. It says, 'Jew Go Home.'"

Tikva gasped. The eyes of the children got wider as they listened.

"This open my eyes. I see that Russia is no good place to be a Jew. I see I need to be a Jew. I leave to come to a Jewish life with good Jewish people. I did not come to find this." The tears in her eyes overflowed and rolled down her cheeks.

Saraleh, seeing Zlata cry, started to bawl. Her screaming scared the baby, who also started to cry. Donny turned to Zahava, who was next to him, and said urgently, over and over, while pulling on her sweater, "I want Ima, I want Ima."

Bracha jumped up to go to the baby and bumped into Yochie, who dropped the robot's remote control, which Chezky stepped on. The robot's tray jumped, sending the peanut butter and jelly flying. Its arms started flailing in the air, banging the bag of bread against the wall. The bag burst open and the bread flew all over the room.

Rivka and Zahava screamed. One piece of bread landed right in the middle of the pie, sending hot mashed potato flying in all directions. Some landed on Moishy, who yelled and ran to the sink to wash off the burning potato.

Moishy's yelling made Saraleh and Rachel Ahuva scream louder. Then Donny started to cry: "Ima! Ima!"

Dina snuck out of the kitchen and ran to the study. With trembling hands, she dialed her mother's work number. The telephone rang three times and someone picked up.

"Hello, Sefer Press," a voice said. *Baruch Hashem,* it was her mother!

"Ima," she began.

"Who is this? I'm very busy right now."

"Ima, please, it's Dina." Dina's voice was low and

trembly. "Please come home."

There was a pause on the other end of the telephone. "Dini, hon, I'm in the middle of a very important meeting, can it wait?"

"No, Ima, it can't. Ima, we need you."

There was another long pause. Then Mrs. Baker said, "Okay, honey, I'm on my way."

11
Ima Comes Home

As Mrs. Shoshana Baker drove carefully and deliberately through the rain, her mind was racing. What could be the problem? What was going on at home? It couldn't be that someone was hurt, *chas veshalom*, Dina would have told me. It must be some crisis for her to sound like that. What could be happening? What could it be? The whispered slap, slap of the windshield wipers accentuated her worried thoughts.

As she pulled around the corner, she thought she saw Zlata in the distance, walking quickly away from the house. Is that Zlata? Why is she leaving now? I thought we agreed that she would stay until one of us got home. Mrs. Baker's heart beat faster.

She pulled the car into the driveway and jumped out, not even bothering to lock up. She ran up the back stairs but instead of rushing in, she stopped and stood for a moment to collect her thoughts.

Through the door she could hear a general commotion. Saraleh was sobbing and Donny moaning. The voices of the quints rose and fell. Forgetting her thought collection, Mrs. Baker burst in the door.

"Ima!"

"Ima's home!"

Saraleh threw herself into her mother's arms and cried out, "Oh, Ima, everyone was crying!" Donny stood looking at her with big, pained, round eyes.

Mrs. Baker surveyed the kitchen. There, on the table was the cooled Shepherd's Pie. Obviously, dinner had started and stopped. Yochie and Chezky were cleaning up the smashed jam jar. Zahava was putting away the peanut butter. Moishy was nursing his burn. Rachel Ahuva was in Bracha's arms, her head nestled against her big sister, her eyes wide. Half of the children's eyes were red from crying and on every face was an expression of misery.

Mrs. Baker turned to Dina. "Well, Dini, you called," she said. "Do you want to tell me what's been happening?"

"Oh, Ima," Rivka burst out before Dina could speak. "Everything's been awful since you went to work!"

"Today was the worst," Yochie put in.

Just then, Mr. Baker breezed in the door. "Hello, everyone," he said cheerily. "Shoshana! I didn't expect you home until later. I'm glad to see dinner is still on the table. Where's Zlata?"

No one could say anything. As he looked around

the room, Mr. Baker realized that things were not as they should be.

"Yes, where's Zlata?" Mrs. Baker asked. "I thought I saw her leaving. Why did she leave early?"

The children stood silent and ashamed. At last, Dina spoke up. "She left...she left because we hurt her feelings." She swallowed hard and tears came to her eyes.

"You hurt her feelings?" Mr. Baker asked. "So much that she had to leave early?"

Dina looked down at her feet and whispered, "Yes."

Mr. and Mrs. Baker looked at each other, bewildered and worried. Mr. Baker cleared his throat. "I see, " he said. "Bracha — no, Bracha is holding the baby — Zahava, please make coffee for your mother and me. Everyone sit down. It's time for a Baker family meeting." Mr. Baker removed his raincoat and hung it over the back of his chair. "Take off your coat Shoshana," he said to his wife.

While Zahava made coffee, the other children took their places at the large kitchen table. Zahava put the coffee down in front of her parents and went to her place. Mr. Baker made a *berachah* and sipped his drink.

"Okay, which one of you feels qualified to tell me what happened?" he asked.

"Dina," said Tikva before anyone could speak. Dina looked alarmed. The children nodded in agreement.

"Okay, Dina, let's hear it."

Dina sat for a minute and collected her thoughts. Then she began. "Well, I don't know how it started. I mean, I guess I do know how it started. Zlata said that she was going to make something new, so when we sat down we were really excited. When we saw that it was potatoes again, we, um, some of us, got very excited, um, upset. A lot of people wouldn't eat. One of us started to make sandwiches. Then...some-one...wrote something on the window." She glanced at the window, which had been cleaned off.

"What was written on the window?"

Dina looked around the room. She didn't want to be the one to say. Chezky mumbled something.

"I beg your pardon?" Mr. Baker asked him.

" 'Zlata go home,' " he repeated a little louder.

Mrs. Baker blanched and looked at her husband. Mr. Baker looked hard at the children.

"Anyway," Dina said quickly, "she was very upset. She told us how she was a scientist in Russia and how the goyim wrote on her door..."

"We know the story," Mr. Baker interrupted.

"Then everything went crazy. Saraleh and the baby cried. Goldie went crazy."

"Goldie?" Mr. Baker asked. "Who's Goldie?"

"The robot," Yochie told him, pointing to the robot standing back in the corner. Mr. Baker looked at the robot for a moment, his mouth twitching. He turned back to Dina. "Go on," he said.

"Moishy got a burn and Donny wanted Ima. I went to call Ima, and when I came back, Zlata was leaving."

"She was crying!" Saraleh said, her big eyes filling up with tears once again.

Mrs. Baker just looked at her children.

"Well," said Mr. Baker. "Well, well, well! Tell me, how do you feel about what happened?" he asked them.

"Awful!" Rivka blurted out.

"Really awful," said Zahava.

"Terrible," said Tikva and hung her head.

"I feel like a real fink," said Chezky.

"At first, I was mad," said Moishy. "But now I'm, well, sad. But I'm sadder for Zlata." He sighed. "Things really aren't the same since Ima went to work."

Mrs. Baker winced.

"I think we have to be careful about blaming things on circumstances," said Mr. Baker. "Each person is responsible for his or her own behavior, no one else." The children hung their heads.

"Well," said Mr. Baker again. "What are we going to do?"

"Do?" Zahava asked. "What can we do?"

"What do you think?"

"We can apologize," said Tikva.

"We could send her a letter," Chezky suggested.

"Maybe a telegram," put in Moishy.

The children thought some more. Suddenly, Yochie sat bolt upright. "Let's send Goldie!"

"Yeah!" said Chezky. "We could put a note in her hand and flowers on the tray! It would be neat!" He stood up to activate the robot and saw his parents' faces. "No," he said, "It's no good. We gotta go our- selves." He sat down and stuffed his hands in his pockets.

"When?" Rivka asked.

"When do you think?" her father asked her.

"Now," she said in a small voice. The other chil- dren solemnly nodded in agreement.

Rivka stood up. "Is it still raining?" she asked. "I'll go and get umbrellas."

"No, it's not raining," her father informed her. "It's cleared up."

"Let's get our coats," said Dina.

Several children left the kitchen.

"But where does she live?" Bracha asked.

"I'll write down the address for you," said Mrs. Baker, standing up. She found a pencil, a piece of paper, and the address book. "It's not far," she said. She handed the paper to Bracha.

"Should we wait in the car?" Moishy asked, pulling on his jacket.

"What for?" his mother asked.

"Aren't you going to drive us?" Moishy looked confused.

"It's within walking distance," Mrs. Baker informed him.

Suddenly, the truth dawned on Moishy. "You mean, you're not coming with us?" The other children, who by this time were back in the kitchen, looked up in surprise. "I mean, I thought..."

Mrs. Baker slowly shook her head.

"Oh," said Moishy.

"How can we go alone?" Zahava wailed softly.

"You managed to do the first part alone..." Mrs. Baker looked steadily at her daughter.

"Oh." Zahava swallowed hard.

One by one, the Baker children said a quiet good-bye and filed out the door. Dina was last. As she passed her mother, she gave her a soft kiss on the cheek. "Bye-bye, Ima," she whispered.

"Bye-bye, *zeeskeit*," said Mrs. Baker. *"Behatz-lachah."*

The kitchen seemed very empty after the children left. The remains of the Shepherd's Pie still sat on the table, cold and lumpy. The faucet dripped. Goldie stood stoicly in her place by the wall, the empty bread bag still dangling from her hand. Rachel Ahuva, who was put in her high chair during the meeting, had fallen asleep and was snoring gently, her head on the tray.

"I'd better put her in her bed," Mrs. Baker said, standing up and going to the baby. She gathered her in her arms and turned toward the door. The robot caught her eye.

"Where did that thing come from?" she asked her husband.

Mr. Baker was thinking, staring with unfocused eyes at a spot just over his empty coffee cup. "Huh?" he said.

"Where did that robot come from?" Mrs. Baker asked again. "I assume it's Moishy's."

"No, it belongs to Yochie and Chezky," Mr. Baker told her. "It's a project for the Science Fair."

"Some project!" Mrs. Baker gave a small laugh. "I'm going to put the baby to bed."

"I'll be in the study," Mr. Baker stretched, rubbed his back and went out.

The baby, exhausted after her exciting day, didn't wake up as Mrs. Baker changed her diaper and put her in pajamas. After tucking her in her crib, she stood up and looked around. Above Saraleh's bed, taped crookedly on the wall, was a crayon drawing of a rain storm. Mrs. Baker chuckled at the gigantic, gray, raindrops and the swirly clouds. "I didn't see this one," she said to herself.

On impulse, she went into Bracha's room. As usual, everything was in order. She wandered over the desk. On top of a pile of books lay the math test and the Chumash test. "One hundred percent," Mrs. Baker said with admiration. "Good old Bracha! Why didn't she tell me?" She looked over the tests for a minute before putting them down.

In the quintuplets' room, she found the usual clutter. Yochie's bed was piled with clothes, books, and tools. "Tools?" Mrs. Baker wondered. "Oh, the robot."

The closet door was open. Mrs. Baker admired Zahava's meticulous arrangement. She remembered that there'd been some sort of problem with the closet. It annoyed her that she couldn't remember exactly what the problem was. Well, the closet certainly looked fine now.

On Zahava's bed was a notebook opened to a page with the title, "Ideas for the Sewing Club" across the top in colorful letters. The page was blank. Mrs. Baker frowned.

On Dina's bed was her diary. Mrs. Baker was always tempted to read this diary in particular, because Dina was usually such a quiet kid, but she never did. She wondered what it said inside, maybe: "Dear Diary. Another day without Ima..."?

In Moishy's room, she found choral music, homework, and other projects scattered around. She was surprised to see that there were no Lego creations on the shelves and wondered why. She found indecipherable notes for his computer program and chuckled. Then she remembered the incident with Ashi and frowned again.

She went down to the kitchen and began to clear up. The kids will need to eat when they get home, but I won't serve this, she thought as she wrapped up the Shepherd's Pie. Not right now, anyway. We can always have eggs.

She stopped in front of the robot. That Yochie, she thought, what will she think of next! This should really wow them at the Science Fair. A Science Fair! I've been so busy it didn't even sink in! Moishy's program and the robot, for the Science Fair."

Mrs. Baker put the casserole dish down on the counter. She leaned back and crossed her arms, deep in thought. Then, coming to a conclusion and making a decision, she marched to the study to speak to her husband.

When the Baker children filed into the house and through the kitchen, chattering and excited, they were a little annoyed to find their mother on the telephone with her boss. They stood around, impatiently waiting for her to finish.

"That's my final decision, Nava.... Yes, I'm sure...I know I'm doing what's right.... Thank-you, Nava, I gotta run. Bye." Mrs. Baker hung up the telephone.

"Ima, we had such a nice talk!" Dina began excitedly.

"Wait!" Mrs. Baker held up one hand. "I want Abba to hear this, too. Go hang up your coats while I get him."

"I'll get him," Moishy volunteered.

Seconds later, a much happier Baker family was sitting around the kitchen table.

"Since Dina told the not-so-good news, she deserves to tell the good stuff, too," Mr. Baker said. Everyone agreed. Mr. Baker indicated that Dina should begin. Dina, flushed and excited, began to talk very quickly.

"Well, we got there and Zahava opened the door..."

"I did not!" Zahava protested.

"I mean Zlata/Zahava," Dina explained.

"Let's call Zlata, Zlata, for the sake of clarity," Mr. Baker suggested.

"Okay," Dina agreed. "So Zlata opened the door. Boy, was she surprised to see us!" Dina stopped for a minute and said soberly. "You could see that she'd been crying...." The children looked uncomfortable. "Anyway," she went on. "She invited us in and we didn't even take off our coats or anything before we apologized. She was very touched and I think she was going to cry again. Then she took out a...a...what do you call it, Tikki?"

"A samovar," Tikva said.

"A samovar," Dina repeated. "And she made really strong tea and she showed us how to drink it through a sugar cube like some people do in Russia."

"Chezky almost choked and he got tea up his nose," Donny said excitedly.

"Donny," Chezky told him. "Don't interrupt."

"Well, we talked a lot and Zlata told us about life in Russia," Dina continued. "Then she asked us about American food and promised to try and cook more American."

"I said I'd help her with recipes," Bracha said.

"I was really impressed that she said that," Tikva put in. "It shows how giving she is." The other Bakers agreed in force.

"And Ima," Zahava said, her eyes glowing. "I found my sewing project. We're going to redecorate her apartment!"

"Are you sure that's all right?" Mrs. Baker looked surprised.

"Oh, Ima!" Zahava exclaimed. "She lives in this tiny, little apartment; it's actually very charming, but she has such old stuff, there are no curtains, and all the chairs are ripped. When I told her the idea, she seemed very happy." Zahava considered for a minute. "She's even doing us a favor, too, if you see what I mean," she said.

"I see your point," Mrs. Baker said dryly.

"We can make it a school-wide project!" Zahava concluded.

"Sounds good to me," Mrs. Baker said with enthusiasm.

"Well, we're proud of all of you," Mr. Baker said, beaming at his family.

"Yes," Mrs. Baker chimed in. "Very proud. It's a big thing to be able to say you're sorry."

"In case you were worried, Ima," said Bracha, "Zlata is coming in tomorrow, so you won't be late for work or anything."

"Thank you, Bracha," said Mrs. Baker, "but I have a little announcement to make."

A little announcement? What could it be? Everyone wondered.

"Well, kids, while you were out, I was thinking," their mother told them. "And I realized that I really miss you and that we really need each other more than I thought. I saw that I've been missing out on a lot of important things, and I have let you down once or twice. I don't think that's how things should be. So, I've made a decision." She looked at Mr. Baker. "I should say, we've made a decision." He nodded at her and winked. She smiled.

"I can't quit work; we do need the money, but we

don't need it as badly and as quickly as we thought we did. I'm cutting down on my hours. I'll be working four mornings a week, when everyone is in school. For the rest of my hours, I'll set up a computer and work at home. It still won't be easy, but I think it will be better. What do you say?"

Yochie let out a long, wild whoop. Moishy shouted "Hurray!" and waved his hands in the air. Jumping up, the children ran and hugged their mother.

"Oh, Ima, it will be so *good* to have you home again!" Dina gushed.

When it was Tikva's turn to hug her mother, she said very softly. "Ima, about that computer...."

"Yes, Tikki?" Mrs. Baker asked.

"Could you set it up in the homework room?"

"In the homework room?" Mrs. Baker was taken aback.

"We won't bother you," Tikva promised. "We just want you near us."

"Why not, Shoshana?" Mr. Baker asked.

"Why not?" Mrs. Baker's expression softened. "Why not!" She gave her daughter another little hug.

"Okay, Tikki," she said. "I'll set up in the homework room — together with my kids."

Coming Up Next In
BAKER'S DOZEN

What do you get when you combine twelve Baker kids, eight days of Pesach, and one luxury hotel?

What do you get when one of those Bakers—16-year-old Ashi—is set on proving his independence by working as a waiter?

What you get, as always, is that wonderful Baker mix of bedlam, laughter, serious lessons, and just plain fun that has made this series so well loved by kids everywhere.

Look for more Baker excitement in *Baker's Dozen #8: Hey, Waiter!*

To order FALLING LETTERS GAME, fill out this coupon and mail to:

TARGUM PRESS
Falling Letters Game
22700 W. Eleven Mile Rd
Southfield, Mich. 48034

Allow 6 to 8 weeks for delivery.

— — — — — — — — — — — — —

YES! I want to enjoy Moishy Baker's terrific new computer game, *Falling Letters*. Please rush me the software and manual so that I can start playing soon!

Please send ☐ 5¼"   ☐ 3½" disk to:

Name _____

Address _____

City_____ State_____ Zip_____

Phone # _____

Enclosed is my check or money order for $19.95.